HEAVEN CAN'T WAIT, OR CAN IT?

The Fruition

HEAVEN CAN'T WAIT, OR CAN IT?

The Fruition

William Porter

ISBN-13: 978-1-944662-51-6

Affirmation Press Publishing date: 08/15/2020

This is a work of fiction based on true events. Names, characters, places and incidents are the product of the author's imagination or are used fictitiously. Any resemblance to actual events, locals, or persons, living or dead, is entirely coincidental.

Cover Design by Michael Scott, MASGraphicarts.com

Acknowledgments

A debt of gratitude is extended to the following for the work done on this project:

Carlos Parks, Illustrator

Michael Scott, Front and back cover producer

Mary Louise Smith, Cover drawings

Diana Henderson, Editor

Affirmation Press: Drew Becker, Publisher

Contents

1. PLANNING THE TRIP

After a good night's sleep, Maggie and Fred woke up teary eyed, still thinking about that starlit night they viewed together through the sky window Fred had installed only weeks earlier.

Still comfortably lying in bed, Maggie said, "Fred, I really enjoyed last night when we looked out of that sky window. I don't know why we didn't install it sooner. And the strange thing is, I can't wait for tonight to come so we can take advantage of it again. To be able to see a starlit sky like we saw last night means so much."

"Yeah, it was really nice," Fred replied.

For Fred and Maggie Mints, heaven had arrived in both of their lives because finally they had each other.

Both Maggie and Fred really enjoyed living in their new house. Of course, it wasn't exactly new to them anymore. They had left the condo downtown and moved into the ranch style home six months earlier.

They were finally healing from the many losses they had known in their lives. The memory of Maggie's parents still crept into her mind on occasion, and her former husband John continued to hold a soft spot in her heart. As for Fred, well, he had certainly gotten over his feelings about Courtney and was thankful to keep her as a friend in whom he still could confide.

Having relocated from Hawaii to Chicago, Fred finally had what he wanted all along—the love of his life, Maggie. He still experienced challenges in his writing career and on his job at Mojco. But now all that didn't matter because he had Maggie.

It was a typical week for both Maggie and Fred. Maggie had her job to do at her daycare, but she had the help that she needed in her niece Mary. As for Fred, an author's job is never done, so he continued to write while becoming more adapted to his new position at Mojco headquarters in Chicago. Now that he had moved from his downtown condo to the suburbs, the traffic presented a challenge for him getting to and from work. He compensated for that problem, however, by meditating on the next story he was going to write when he was stuck in the bumper-to-bumper commute. The responsibilities of his job had increased since his return from Hawaii, so the stop and go driving allowed for more than enough time to think about that as well.

On weekends Maggie and Fred found time to relax a little. They took advantage of their spacious fenced backyard and the enclosure attached to the back of their home. Although the screened-in area was similar to Fred's condo back in Hawaii, it didn't provide the spectacular view with the Pacific Ocean serving as a backdrop. He had enough of that anyway—even though he still thought about the times when Courtney visited him there and the many conversations they shared. While not as magnificent as the scenery from the beach condo in Hawaii, the view of the greenery in their backyard from the porch of their current home provided a serenity that both Maggie and Fred needed at this time in their lives.

The highlight of their weekend, other than their weekly attendance at church, was the social gathering that they had with Courtney and Gates Manley. The Mints and the Manleys had become inseparable couples. They entertained each other on most Sunday evenings. These social occasions gave all four of them an opportunity to put the previous workweek behind them so they could begin the new week feeling renewed.

§ § §

It was not the week's activities that Maggie looked forward to the most. At the end of every day, she anticipated the joy of viewing the stars through their sky window. A usual day at home was filled with chores galore, and she welcomed those precious moments of star gazing.

One evening Fred returned home from one of his writer's conferences and went straight to bed. When Maggie retired after a long day of work at the daycare, as she had done for several evenings, she opened the sky window and, while lying on her back, looked through it to view the multitude of stars that glittered in the night time sky. She just stared at them, wondering what the future would bring.

As Fred lay there beside her, he asked, "Mag, you really love that sky window, don't you?"

"Yes, Fred, I do. It helps me sleep soundly."

"Well, I'm counting on that," he said, "because I'm really tired after everything I've done today." In no uncertain terms, he added, "So don't wake me up. And I'm looking forward to a hot breakfast tomorrow morning!"

Before long he drifted off to sleep, leaving her to contemplate the future as she continued to gaze at the stars. After a while she too drifted off into the abyss of slumber, but soon a long and thorough dream emerged in her unconsciousness.

Figure 1. Maggie Looking through the Sky Window

"The heavens declare the glory of God; and the firmament shows His handiwork." (Psalm 19:1)

In the dream she was playing bingo, a game she loved to play after their usual Sunday evening meal. Usually they dined by themselves, but this time the Mints and Manleys had a few neighbors over to participate.

At the end of one game, Gates offered an appealing suggestion to everyone there: "You guys, the hotel chain I'm with is offering complimentary cruise tickets for Courtney and me and three other couples. Now how about that? Would any of you be interested?"

Maggie spoke up quickly and said, "Of course we would! Wouldn't you, honey?" she asked hoping Fred would give a positive response, which he did.

"Yeah, it's something that would be very relaxing. But we're just one couple. Who would be the other two couples that would join us?" Fred asked Gates.

Since none of the other people at the table offered a positive response to Gates' proposition, Maggie said, "Well, if no one else here would like to go, I know my friend Sandra would love to go on a trip like that, and she could partner with my college friend Katie. And there may be another couple I'm thinking about too."

"Well, I guess it's all set," Gates said.

One of the others at the table made a statement that was probably representative of all the others there who did not express an interest. He said, "I know I'll be working," and most of the others present nodded their heads in agreement.

Maggie asked Gates, "By the way, where are we going?"

"Well, we have to decide on three options for the trip—Alaska, Jamaica, or Bermuda," Gates replied.

Maggie interrupted Gates again, and said, "One of the options is Bermuda?"

She hoped that would be Gates' choice because Sandra's friend lived there. Maggie began to make her case for that destination.

"You know, Gates, my friend Sandra went to Bermuda and had a wonderful time there. Let's consider that place."

"Are you kidding me? I was thinking the same thing. That would be perfect," Gates responded. "Is everyone good with that? Except, of course, those who can't go because of work," Gates asked.

He saw that both Courtney and Fred nodded their heads in approval, so it was confirmed that the Mints plus Maggie's friend Sandra and her college roommate could be two of the three couples that Gates would invite. Meanwhile, all the others at the table just sat there, hoping that Gates would propose a trip again later when they would be able to go.

Gates focused his comments on Maggie and Fred since they had agreed to go. "But there are still two other things that we have to clear up," he said. "First of all, we need at least one more couple, because the special that my company is giving requires four couples to participate."

Again Maggie spoke up. "Well, I can tell you, Gates, my friend Katie has a teenager, and, since our trip could be when school is out, he can go too. Yeah, she has a son whose name is Wynn. If you add Sandra's Bermuda friend Erin, that would make up the fourth pair you need."

Gates said, "Okay, I'll see if we could make that work. Of course, I'll have to get the approval of my hotel's administration."

Maggie replied, "Okay, Gates. While you're checking on that, I'll call Sandra to see if she's interested. But I know her; she will be ecstatic!"

After that, Maggie took a bathroom break and continued to consider the trip more seriously. *Yeah, I think we can make all this work. And the more I think about it, the more I think that it will work. Katie's son Wynn and Sandra's friend Erin can make that third pair, and hopefully Erin can entertain us while we're in Bermuda, but I'll confirm that when I talk with Sandra. She'll be able to contact Erin about the arrangements we're planning, and, knowing what Sandra has told me about her, I think she would like what we're trying to do.*

As Maggie pondered all these considerations, she held hope that all would fall into place. After her little conversation with herself, she felt refreshed and returned to the bingo game with her friends.

Meanwhile Gates confirmed with his hotel's administration the arrangement they were making would be okay. He told Maggie by phone the next day that all the details were approved.

He continued, "Tomorrow I'll formally submit all the necessary forms to my hotel administration, so everything will be set."

"That's great, Gates," Maggie responded. "I'll tell Fred that everything is a go for the cruise."

§ § §

Gates and Courtney and Maggie and Fred had a new sense of purpose over the next several months. They each worked on planning for the cruise and notifying the other affected parties. Maggie knew the others would be equally excited about this trip.

Maggie couldn't wait to tell Sandra about their plans. She was sure Sandra would be willing to come.

Maggie said to Fred, "Let me give Sandra a call to tell her about our plans."

"Okay, but make sure you give her all the details she needs in order to make a good decision."

Before Maggie had a chance to talk to Sandra, she gave Gates a call to get some more information about the trip. As they were talking, Gates asked Maggie a question.

"By the way, Maggie, where is this college roommate of yours located?"

"Katie lives with her son in New York."

"New York?" Gates responded. "Why, that's where we're leaving from. Well, how about that! Hey, everything is really falling into place! Our ship leaves out of the New York harbor, and we could pick up your college roommate just before we get on the ship. Not only that, but we could spend some time having fun in the Big Apple before we board. And by the way, we *will* be going to Bermuda."

The joy that Maggie felt after that conversation with Gates could not be measured. Soon after that, Maggie gave Sandra a call to tell her about the plans they had made for the cruise.

"Hello, Sandra. How are you doing?"

"I'm fine, Maggie," Sandra replied. Maggie continued, "Well, listen, before you say much of anything, I have some good news for you. I think that it's something that you won't be able to refuse. It's something really wonderful."

"Oh, come on now! Come on! Maggie, please don't tease me! What is it?" Sandra asked, anxious to hear the news.

Maggie finally told her, "You know, Sandra, Gates and Courtney were over to our house to have dinner as they often do on Sunday evenings. Well, this time as we were playing bingo, Gates invited us to come along with them on a cruise that his hotel chain is putting on for couples."

Sandra interrupted. "Okay, how does that involve me? Don't get me wrong, I'm very excited for you, Maggie. You know how much I told you I enjoyed my trip to Bermuda when I took it the other summer. Of course, at that time I flew and didn't have the luxury of taking my time on a cruise like you and Fred are going to do."

"Okay, can I finish, Sandra?" Maggie asked with growing impatience.

Sandra responded, "Well, go ahead, Maggie."

"It's not just me and Fred who Gates invited to come along with him; it was two other couples too."

"Okay, I get it, but that leaves me out again, Maggie, because this cruise is apparently for couples only, and as you know I'm a single woman."

"But you don't understand, Sandra," Maggie interjected. "I invited you to come along with us, and Gates approved!" Maggie continued, "And before you interrupt me again, let me explain. I mentioned to him that you, your friend Erin, my old college roommate Katie and her teenage son could make up the two couples. Now before you respond, just let me also say that all expenses are taken care of. Now how does that sound to you?"

Sandra responded, "Well, that sounds great! Yeah, Maggie, I'm now getting it. I'm going on a cruise! Oh, Maggie, I'm so excited."

"That's my girl," Maggie said, relieved she finally understood and was in full agreement with coming along on the cruise.

"Well, where will we be cruising to?" Sandra asked.

"We're going to Bermuda. Yeah, we're cruising to Bermuda," Maggie said with a smile. Sandra was speechless for a few seconds. Maggie immediately wondered if her friend was okay.

"Are you still there, Sandra?"

"Oh, yes, I'm still here, Maggie. I'm just overwhelmed by what you are telling me. You mean I can go back to Bermuda on a cruise with you and your friends?"

"Yes, that's exactly what I'm telling you, Sandra," Maggie replied.

Figure 2: Woman on the Phone

"You have turned for me my mourning into dancing; You have put off my sackcloth and clothe me with gladness." (Psalm 30:11)

Sandra screamed right there on the phone. "Yes, yes, yes! I'm going back to Bermuda. I can't believe it. Maggie, I'm filled with emotion right now. I don't think I can contain it. To be going back to Bermuda after the time I had there is just too much. Listen, Maggie, we'll be talking about this more as the time for our departure approaches. But let me ask you this now: when is the cruise scheduled to depart?"

After hearing Sandra's excitement, Maggie replied, "It will depart during the first week of June this coming summer."

"Maggie, that's great, because I had enrolled in a business course at the local technical college, but that won't start until later in the summer. Oh, I can't wait to contact my friend Erin in Bermuda to let her know I'm coming there to see her again, and this time with some friends of mine."

Maggie said, "That's great, Sandra, because I was going to ask you to call her to see if she was agreeable to all of us coming."

"Don't worry about that. I'll talk to her," Sandra said. "And even if she's cool to the idea, I'll convince her to say yes to everything. But I really don't think I'll have to do that. Anyway, thank you so much Maggie. But right now, I have to go to work, and I'll be talking with you later."

"Okay, Sandra. I knew you'd be excited about it," Maggie said. With that, the conversation between Maggie and Sandra ended.

§ § §

Sandra was so excited about her trip back to Bermuda that she gave Erin a call immediately after finishing talking with Maggie. It didn't matter that she'd be a little late for work. Erin had done so much for her during that time she was on the island. She remembered it as though it was only yesterday. Erin had encouraged her to look for specific signs that God was speaking to her. With her limited spiritual knowledge at the time, it wasn't easy for her to fully comprehend such spiritual insights. But Sandra realized that she was in a desperate situation, both having to overcome a serious car accident as well as being diagnosed with a terminal illness. When Maggie told Sandra of the invitation to travel with the group to Bermuda, she naturally felt excited.

As far as the accident was concerned, it came during a time when Sandra was intending to do something that surely God would not approve of: getting involved with another woman's husband. Yes, she was on her way to see Fred, who was attending a conference in Minneapolis. She had found a way to be there to see him, hoping for a romantic rendezvous. But thank God she had come to her senses. She had seen the light largely as a result of the accident and thanks to Erin's advice. Sandra received some godly wisdom during her time at Erin's resort in Bermuda; she ended up using that advice long after she had left the island. It was as if God knew that she needed what she got—wise counsel from someone who believed that God can turn any situation, any problem around. Erin had helped Sandra deal with two storms in her life, her illness and her recovery and rehabilitation from the car accident. Sandra received this wisdom as a literal storm of nature came and went on the islands, providing a starlit sky that was critical in Sandra's renewal. After that sign she knew that she too would overcome her personal storms thanks to Erin's advice.

But Erin would be the first to say that it really wasn't by her efforts that Sandra overcame her difficulties. It was by the intervention of the Holy Spirit in her life during that time. And now Sandra would have a chance for her friends to experience a place that was a pivotal turning point in her life. She saw it as an opportunity to share a newfound faith, a faith that can move mountains.

REFERENCE

So Jesus answered and said to them, "Assuredly, I say to you, if you have faith and do not doubt, you will not only do what was done to the fig tree, but also if you say to this mountain, 'Be removed and be cast into the sea,' it will be done. And whatever things you ask in prayer, believing, you will receive."
(Matthew 21:21-22)

2. TO THE BIG APPLE

Over the months since Gates first offered the proposal for going on a cruise, all involved had steadily planned for the big day. Maggie and Fred, Maggie's friend Katie, and Sandra, who would presumably partner with Erin once they arrived on Bermuda, seemed thrilled at the idea. Everyone except Katie's son Wynn looked forward to the trip.

Wynn was a rebel of sorts. He never got over his father leaving his mother to raise him alone. Wynn remembered being close to his father before he left. But suddenly he was gone. Over the years a lot of resentment had built up in Wynn because of his father's departure from their lives.

Katie did an excellent job as a single parent. Wynn had developed into a good student. In fact, he became president of his sophomore class when he entered high school. But somehow, he got involved with a wayward crowd that led him astray. He even spent some time in juvenile detention for throwing rocks at passing cars when he and a small group of other boys were messing around under a bridge one day. So he really needed the trip to clear his head but was lukewarm about the idea to say the least. In fact, he did everything he could to justify not going. But Wynn loved the beach, so he reluctantly agreed to go.

While Gates and Courtney arranged the trip through his company, they left the details for planning the venture to Maggie. They became known as "Maggie's group." She had already contacted Sandra, who in turn had called Erin to let her know of the arrangements. Maggie also contacted her college roommate Katie and gave her all the details about what she would need on the trip including the date and time of departure from the New York port.

Maggie would accomplish the planning over the next several weeks and prepare to leave Detroit with husband Fred and her friend Sandra, who would ride with them to the big city. Sandra could not contain her joy and continued to anticipate the trip. Maggie's old roommate Katie and her son Wynn would be waiting for them when they arrived in New York for departure on the *Rhythm of the High Seas*, the cruise ship that would house them for the journey.

After months of planning, the big day was only one week away. Early that Monday morning, Maggie gave Sandra a call.

"Hello, Sandra. How are you doing this morning?"

"I'm fine Maggie," Sandra replied.

"Sandra, the reason I'm calling so early in the morning is because I had a thought about our upcoming trip, and I didn't want to forget to ask you. Anyway, are you getting prepared for the big trip? I know we still have a week to go before we leave, but you know how I am. I'm a perfectionist about certain things, and I want to make sure you are getting yourself prepared. It's such a major trip. And you know it's never too early to make sure you have everything."

Sandra replied, "Yeah, I know, Maggie. You're usually on top of everything. But to answer your question, yes, I'm getting ready for the trip."

"Well, I'm glad to hear that you're getting ready." Maggie continued, "And I'm glad you feel the way you do about everything. You know we all have to have the time frame that we're working with for this vacation. So remember, Sandra, we'll be gone for nine days beginning Monday a week from today, and we'll be away until Tuesday of the following week. The actual cruise is seven days, but we'll have all day that Monday to have some fun in the Big Apple before we depart on the cruise ship the next day on Tuesday. We'll spend Tuesday night and Wednesday cruising and be on the ship for a second night before we arrive in Bermuda on Thursday. We'll be in Bermuda Thursday night, all day Friday and Saturday, and then we'll depart for Little Fiji island on Sunday morning. I don't think that I mentioned it, but this stopover is just a little bit extra that the hotel administration Gates is working with is awarding us. It should be nice. This small extra on the trip will also give us time to recover from our stay in Bermuda. Anyway, we'll make this stopover that Monday and return to New York on Tuesday to complete the trip. When we arrive back, on that day we'll drive to Detroit later in the afternoon. Whew! What a trip it's going to be, wouldn't you say, Sandra?"

Sandra was momentarily speechless after that rather detailed description of the time frame for the trip. But she came around to answer, "Maggie, you're so detailed. It seems as though you have everything covered on this trip."

"Well, I'm trying, Sandra. I guess it's in my genes, and you can thank my mother Mensie for that," Maggie replied. She added, "Yeah, so we can come by to pick you up. I know you don't want to drive all the way to New York by yourself. You can ride with me and Fred to the Big Apple."

Maggie and Fred were ready to go, and Maggie especially was overjoyed about the trip. But there was still another week left before they would take off. The week before they were to leave for New York to board the cruise dragged by slowly for Maggie.

§ § §

It had been a long cold winter, and everyone was looking forward to the beginning of summer at the beach. Even in New York City, the temperatures in early June were only a few degrees higher than they were in Detroit. Detroit was farther west and at a higher latitude than New York. Being farther south and on the Atlantic was an advantage during late spring and early summer for the nation's largest city, where temperatures became mild.

The day of their departure was finally upon them. Maggie, Fred, and Sandra set off for New York. It was a cool, clear day as the early rising sun started to warm things up. After a largely uneventful drive from Detroit with Fred behind the wheel, it was shortly after noontime when they approached the Hudson River from the west with the city's massive skyline hovering over the water. The almost constant and steady drive on the interstate gave way to a buildup in traffic as they approached the midtown tunnel. For security reasons, there were several check points as they neared the tunnel. Traffic slowed considerably as every vehicle was screened before proceeding through the famous passageway to the nation's largest city. Fortunately, they had stopped for breakfast about an hour earlier at a pancake restaurant off the interstate.

After normal checks just prior to entering the tunnel, they were allowed to enter this dark, narrow passageway into the canyons of Manhattan. They eventually emerged from the blackness of the tunnel into midtown Manhattan surrounded by traffic jams, herds of people walking everywhere, and the shadows of skyscrapers all around them dimming the scene along the streets on what was otherwise a perfectly clear, sunny day.

After a long drive from Detroit, Fred began to traverse the western part of Manhattan Island as he meandered through the now stop-and-go traffic. They drove past Broadway, not very far from Times Square. The driving was slow, so there was ample opportunity for Maggie and Sandra to see the sights and to witness what might be called organized confusion. The best Fred could do was to navigate through the crowded city streets without having an accident. So much was going on around them. Both motorists and pedestrians needed to pay attention.

They finally arrived at the eastern Manhattan docks, where the cruise ships typically departed. Maggie, Fred and Sandra would depart on one of those ships the next day when the Rhythm of the High Seas set off for Bermuda. Once they arrived at their place of lodging, they could view the cruise ships that were docked from their hotel balcony high above the city streets below near the top floor of the hotel's 50-story tower.

**Figure 3: New York City Skyline at Midday Viewed
from Beyond the Hudson River**

**"The Lord shall reserve your going out
and your coming in From this time forth,
and even forevermore." (Psalm 121:8)**

Figure 4: Street Scene in New York City

"The Earth is the Lord's and all its fullness, The world and those who dwell therein." (Psalm 24:1)

When they got to the hotel, the first people Maggie saw were Katie and her son.

"Katie! Come on over here and give me a hug," Maggie said greeting her with excitement.

"Maggie, you look as good as ever. Let me introduce you to my son Wynn. I know you've seen him before, but that was when he was a lot younger—probably around thirteen if I recall."

"Hello, Wynn," Maggie said. "Nice to see you again. I know you're going to have a good time."

"Yeah, Ms. Maggie," Wynn replied. "I've heard a lot about you from my mother. But I remember you coming to our house a long time ago. And I remember you telling me how angry you thought I was."

Maggie replied, "I hope you're doing better with that, Wynn. You seem so nice now. Now don't get me wrong. You were nice then; you just had to deal with some things like a lot of kids at that age do."

Katie interjected, "Yeah, Maggie; he's doing a lot better now. So, Maggie, we go way, way back, you know."

Maggie responded, "You know, I know that girl!" She continued, "Yeah, we did quite a bit back in college. Those sure were the days. Anyway, I can't wait to tell everyone about what's in store for later today and for tonight. It's so nice today, so sunny and all, but, you know, the night is coming, and we have so much to do."

"Yeah, Maggie. I'm glad you invited us to go on this trip," Katie said.

Maggie emphasized that while having fun in New York, the main objective of the trip was the cruise, but that wouldn't take place until tomorrow. So she said, "I know that the focus of our being here is on that cruise, but, listen, we can take advantage of our stay here in the city too. There's so much to do. So the remainder of the day, we're going to have such a good time. The party is right here in the middle of New York City," Maggie concluded.

Maggie had planned everything long before their arrival to Ferris Hotel. In addition to the prospect of cruising, she was thrilled about meeting and talking with her college roommate Katie again. She couldn't wait to converse with all the others invited to come along on this trip as well. She had scheduled several activities—mostly non-paying events like shopping and sightseeing in the vicinity of the hotel—for later in the afternoon and evening.

Standing with everyone in the lobby of the hotel, Maggie blurted out, "Hey, everyone, we can eat lunch here at the hotel. I've researched it and the food is good and the prices are reasonable. We can go to our separate rooms to get some rest for about an hour or two. But at 3:00 there's a festival going on in Central Park, which is only about a ten-minute walk from where Gates and Courtney are staying near Times Square."

Katie said, "Hey, everyone. A taxi could take us from here to where Gates and Courtney are staying in no time. we can all walk to the park from there." After thinking about it, Katie added, "Well, it might take two taxis."

Regardless of how they would arrive, they would be serenaded by beach music. When Wynn heard this from Maggie, he was disappointed because he certainly didn't like beach music. He was a fan of the most current popular songs, mainly rock 'n' roll with a little bit of country. Katie had always wondered where Wynn got an interest in country music, but he had some unusual musical tastes from her perspective.

Wynn ended up telling his mother, "Mom, you all can go, but I think I'll stay in the room and get some rest."

"Now, Wynn, you don't know how much fun it is. I know it's not the kind of music that you're accustomed to hearing, but sometimes it's good to hear something different, something that's new to your ears. Oh, come on now; come and go with us."

After his mother's persistent urging, Wynn finally caved in and agreed to come along.

Everyone eventually checked into the hotel and got situated in their rooms. Maggie had taken all the paperwork relating to the reservation she had received from Gates to the hotel's administrative office. She made sure that everyone had gotten to where they were supposed to be.

"Hey, everybody, I know it's been a long trip so far, but we've only gotten as far as New York City. At least we're here at the hotel and checked in. Whew! I'm sure glad of that! And Katie, I'm so happy you decided to come along with us, because you know so much about this place, New York, I mean. And thanks for giving that information on the taxi. We definitely need a way to get from here to where the Manleys are because their hotel is so close to the park."

Maggie continued, "By the way, Katie, how long have you and Wynn been living here?"

Katie replied, "It's been about seven years now, Maggie, and I've missed being in Detroit so much, especially times when we were back in college. Remember those days?"

"Do I remember? Girl, of course I remember," Maggie responded. "That's where my life really got started on the campus of MCCU and in particular that night, oh boy, that night when I met Fred, you know, at that social after the basketball game?"

"Well, well. I'm glad you remember that, Mag," Fred interjected as he was listening to their conversation from nearby.

Katie said to both Maggie and Fred, "You two were such a nice couple, Maggie, when you introduced Fred to me and Corey."

"Fred, Corey was our roommate if you remember."

"Of course, I remember Corey," Fred said. He added, "Katie, have you heard from her?"

"No, I'm afraid not. We've kind of lost touch with one another."

In keeping with the jovial mood everyone was having at the time, Katie jokingly said to Fred, "You know, Fred, let me tell you, Maggie's fortunate that she got to you first!"

"Now, Katie, you know that I've always had eyes only for Mag ever since I saw her that night." Fred added, "Listen to me: I'm not going to tell you what we talked about on the dance floor that night as we serenaded to the music of Gladys Knight, but I will say it had something to do with you."

"Oh, come on, Fred," Katie replied. "You've gotta tell me. I'm all curious now. Please tell me what it was?" Katie pleaded.

Fred replied, "Now, Katie, you know that I'm not going to tell you our secrets. And don't you go to Mag and try to get information from her either. We have an understanding to keep some things to ourselves."

"Well, okay," Katie responded.

Maggie jumped into the discussion and said, "Enough of this jabbering back and forth, you two. We all need to get to our rooms to get some rest. I'll tell you, there's going to be lots to do later this afternoon and into the evening."

So everyone parted ways, going to their separate rooms: Maggie and Fred, Katie and Wynn, and Sandra had her own room. They would meet up with Gates and Courtney, who were staying at another hotel near Times Square, later.

After a quick lunch and some rest, Maggie's group, minus Courtney and Gates, reassembled back in the lobby of the hotel. Only Wynn remained behind because he overslept. Everyone carried on casual conversation as they awaited his arrival. They all were ready to go to their first event of the day.

When Katie finally saw her son coming into the lobby, she said, "Come on in here, fellow. We're ready to go."

"Sorry, Mom. Sorry I overslept. But I'm ready."

Instead of taking a taxi as they had discussed, they rode in a shuttle from their hotel to the one where Courtney and Gates were staying. After arriving, they waited in the lobby for the Manleys to join them.

"Hello, everyone," Gates said to the group as he and Courtney entered.

"Hello, Gates and Courtney," Maggie said. "We've been here for a few minutes, but we're ready to go now to this concert in Central Park.

Courtney replied, "Well, let's go! And we can shake a leg while we're at it!"

So they all went out together through a side entrance of the hotel, and suddenly they were among thousands of people on the crowded sidewalks of Manhattan. Katie lived on Long Island, where she could give her son a more suburban environment, so it was Wynn's first time in this borough of the city that New York is known for—amidst all the skyscrapers, traffic, and crowded sidewalks. Wynn never got a chance to come to this part of the city.

Gates realized he was scheduled to be at another engagement at that time in another part of the hotel. So he said suddenly, "Courtney, I just remembered we have this meeting to attend right now. I'm so sorry, Maggie, but we'll join you guys at the concert a little later."

Maggie was never delighted when her plans went awry but decided to go with the flow. "Well, okay, Gates," she said. "You and Courtney go ahead and do what you have to do, and we'll see you over at the park later. We'll be sitting near the front, and we'll save you seats," she assured them.

Minus Courtney and Gates, Maggie and the rest of her group went to the hotel restaurant for a bite to eat before leaving for the concert. After about fifteen minutes there, Maggie received a called from Gates.

He said, "Hey, Maggie. Are you all about to go to the event over here near the park?"

"Yeah, Gates, we're getting ready to leave now."

"Well, they cancelled the meeting we were going to, so we can meet you here at the hotel before you leave."

"Okay, Gates," she replied. "That's great. We're just now finishing eating, and we can meet you in the lobby where we were a few minutes ago."

So Maggie's group lingered within the hotel lobby, and, after a few minutes, Courtney and Gates approached them.

"Okay, everybody. I think we're ready to go now. I'm ready to party, to listen to some good music!" he said.

Everyone left the hotel through a side entrance as Katie led the way because she knew the way to Central Park, where the festival was taking place. They all took the four-block walk. Katie was a fast walker, so it was difficult for some in the group to keep up with her. Maggie, Fred, and Sandra kept pace with her reasonably well as did Gates and Courtney. But Wynn was different story. His focus strayed to the world around him as he gaped at the architecture of the skyscrapers. Wynn tried to avoid people walking in the opposite direction. He was so intrigued with his surroundings that he fell farther and farther behind as they proceeded to their destination.

Numerous small restaurants and pubs that were dimly lit inside could be seen along with small shops and brightly illuminated convenience stores that were filled with patrons. Many seemed to be taking a reprieve from the constant crowd and noise outside as well as from the extreme high temperatures on this warm, sunny day. Beyond the shadows of the tall buildings, primarily at pedestrian crossings at intersections, sunlight pierced through the shade from the skyscrapers and onto the street. Otherwise, within most of a typical block, sunlight was held at bay by the shadows, making it appear much darker at midday and lessening the intensity of the heat.

Street traffic moved so slowly that to Wynn it seemed to take forever for motorists to get to their destinations. Horns blew frequently signifying drivers' frustration, and sirens from emergency vehicles sounded from multiple directions. Amidst the clatter of people and vehicles in this urban street scene, Wynn felt fortunate to live with his mother in the more serene setting of Long Island.

§ § §

After the group walked for another three or four blocks, they crossed a major boulevard and entered the park. Suddenly the brick and concrete of the city's physical landscape gave way to the nature of Central Park with its abundant greenery including trees, shrubbery, and flowering plants. Even birds could be heard chirping in the trees. To Wynn, it was still not like Long Island, but they had finally gotten away from all the hustle and bustle that New York City is known for. The noise diminished as well as the density of people. And activity slowed to a relaxed pace in the park.

By now it was 3:30 in the afternoon with the sun beaming. Maggie's group was surrounded by trees instead of buildings and concrete. As they progressed into the park, the sounds of melodious voices and raging musical instruments overwhelmed the quieter song of the birds. The melodies were coming from performers at Rumsey Playfield, where the show was beginning. Katie led everyone to what seemed to be a perfect spot to view the artists; they had a clear view of the stage—only five rows of seats away. Before they arrived, they had to get their lawn chairs and, while they had the opportunity, purchase some refreshments from a nearby food stand.

Soon everyone was comfortably seated and ready to enjoy the opening act. Quickly the whole area behind them filled with patrons anticipating a good show. The first performers were progressive country, which thrilled Wynn because he was a country music fan. He had not heard of progressive country, so he was eager to listen to the songs from these local artists. After that, several groups arrived and sang beach music to the crowd's delight.

Figure 5: People Dancing in front of Concert Stage

"This is the day the Lord hath made; We will rejoice and be glad in it."
(Psalm 118:24)

Despite enjoying the concert, the real thrill of the vacation would not come until the next day, when all of them would be on a cruise ship headed towards Bermuda. Nonetheless, they looked forward to the main act, Chairmen of the Board, popular among beach artists in the city.

Soon, the main act took the stage, and it was hard for everyone present to remain in their seats.

"Come on, everybody. Let's get up and dance a little," Maggie encouraged. "We don't have to move from our spot."

So everyone got up and, like most attending the show, danced without restraint.

Maggie and Fred stepped away from the group to get more refreshments. When they returned to the entrance of the venue, they gazed into each other's eyes with joy. They marveled at how much fun everyone was having. The two of them were having the time of their lives on this sunny afternoon in the park.

As sunset approached and twilight fell on them, temperatures dropped almost to the point where a light jacket was needed.

Behind the crowd the city's skyline rose, and the glare of car lights and flashing neon signs awaited them. The day transitioned and the glitter that represented life in New York City became visible.

What a perfect prelude to their cruise this day had been. Maggie had made reservations at a restaurant in the middle of New York City just beyond Times Square near the hotel where Courtney and Gates stayed. After that, the reminder of the night would be spent preparing for their departure the next day.

REFERENCE

"For you shall go out with joy, and be led out with peace; The mountains and the hills Shall break forth into singing before you, And all the trees of the field shall clap their hands." (Isaiah 55:12)

3. CRUISING!

After a full day in the Big Apple on Monday, Maggie and her friends had a hearty breakfast at the hotel on the morning of their departure. Afterward everyone was packed and ready to take a shuttle the short distance to the dock where they were eager to be on their way to Bermuda. Their cruise ship would depart later that afternoon and wouldn't return until a week later. Soon the hustle and bustle of the city would give way to a more serene environment on board when many activities awaited them. The eight-day cruise would be something they all would remember for a long time. But the real experience would not come until they reached their destination, the island of Bermuda.

The hour finally arrived when everyone began boarding, a rather long and laborious process but well worth effort and time.

"Wow, what a large ship," Wynn said as they approached the huge ocean liner.

Maggie gazed at the huge windows on the side of the vessel that appeared to be at least as high as a four-story building. The dining tables covered in crisp white linens were clearly in view as she peered through the windows. She imagined herself formally dressed, sitting at one of those tables as she enjoyed an exquisite meal while cruising in the middle of the ocean.

A more immediate concern for Maggie as well as all the other soon-to-be cruisers was the huge crowd ready to board with her and the group.

Sandra was excited to be boarding a cruise ship since she last came to Bermuda by plane. She commented to Maggie while standing next to her.

"Yeah, it's a lot different from flying where it's so congested."

Wynn's comment about the size of the ship prompted a response from Sandra, who remembered clearly all the congestion at the airport when she first made the trip to Bermuda. At the time she couldn't believe all those people could fit on one jet.

Everyone who arrived at the dock boarded the ship in stages and in alphabetical order. Members of Maggie's group were separated within a huge sheltered area until they came back together just prior to when everyone was to board ship. It took them over an hour for everyone to get on board.

Figure 6: People Board the Ship

"God does not show favoritism."
(Romans 2:11)

Maggie said to Fred, "I've never seen so many people. And the interesting thing is that no one knows anybody else unless they're together with someone they signed up to be with like we are."

"Yeah, that's interesting, Mag," Fred replied. "But let me tell you, not knowing any of these other people, we're not aware of all their differences. I've been thinking, Mag, this is the way God looks at people—people just being people—without identifying them based on how they look or how much or how little money they have or what their personality might be. They're just people to God. Yeah, He's only interested in their knowledge of and response to Him and how genuine they are in treating others."

As they stood in line for what felt like hours, Maggie said, "Well, Fred, that's a good point. Yeah, unless it's identical twins, no two people are alike. We all have our unique identity. And I've read somewhere that even identical twins have some differences that frequently can't be recognized by anyone else. The great thing is that even when we meet and become acquainted with someone, we still might not know their inner feelings—what's deep down in their hearts. But God knows. He knows all about us. And that's why we can come to Him and asked for desires we might have, and He will answer. Truly amazing."

Fred added, "Well, that's true, Mag, but His answer might not be what we want. You know sometimes He says 'no' to something that we might want, because He knows that it's not the best thing for us."

Maggie responded, "Well, that's true, Fred. And I guess that's when we need to trust that things are happening for our good whether or not we get those things we want."

The line they stood in began to move faster and soon they had completed the boarding process.

Knowing they likely would be separated upon boarding the ship, everyone in Maggie's group agreed to reassemble in the ship's main lobby to find out each other's room numbers. One by one each of them meandered around the ship looking for their rooms.

§ § §

When lodging reservations were made, Gates tried his best to get rooms as close to one another as possible. But the quality of accommodations varied considerably for group members, so they ended up being scattered all over the ship. Gates was able to get an expensive suite because of his affiliation with the hotel management who sponsored the program. He and Courtney were in a suite high above almost everything else on the ship. They had a panoramic view of the top portion of the vessel and the expanse of the ocean in all directions, and they took full advantage. From their room's patio, they could see the surfing deck, swimming pool area, and even an outdoor cinema located on the opposite end of the vessel. Most amazing of all, they had a view of the ocean in all directions as it met the horizon.

The room where Maggie and Fred resided was located on a lower level near the middle of the ship at quite a distance from where Courtney and Gates were staying. But the advantage in Maggie's location was that it was where many of the activities were; and they were only steps away from the top deck where there were lounging chairs with a panoramic view of the ocean. In addition to that, there was a huge swimming pool in that area where a live band often performed, playing all kinds of music, and they were near the main dining area.

Sandra was the only one with a single room since Katie and her son Wynn had their room together. Both Sandra and Katie had rooms near the end on the opposite side of ship from where Courtney and Gates were located. They talked a lot at every opportunity and decided that it would be best for the two of them to room together and give Wynn a room to himself. Wynn certainly didn't object to that, so he got the room that he and his mother had booked, and Katie moved in with Sandra. As for Wynn, he saw it as an opportunity to finally be totally by himself.

§ § §

It took a while for everyone to unpack and think about what they wanted to do next. But Maggie didn't give them that opportunity. She had the whole evening planned. After a little rest from the unpacking and getting familiar with accommodations, everyone reassembled in the open lounge area where they first boarded the ship. Once everyone was together again, they all wondered what was coming next.

"Maggie, you're leading us. So now lead us right into that cafeteria. I'm hungry," Sandra said in jest.

Sandra was a jokester. She loved having fun, but she sometimes took things too far. Her idea of enjoyment in the past had included trying to arrange a romantic relationship with Maggie's new husband Fred. That escapade took a near fatal turn when she had an automobile accident on the way to meet him. It took this disaster and learning of what she thought was a terminal illness to prevent her involvement with Fred from happening. Thankfully, the experience she had with her friend Erin the last time she was in Bermuda changed her life.

Maggie replied loudly enough for all in the group to hear her. "Okay, Sandra, we're all going to eat in just a little bit. But we need to talk now about what we're going to do afterwards."

Gates interjected, "You all do know there's going to be a great show happening tonight in the main auditorium, right? I've researched it. It's Saxophonist Kenny G and his Endless Amour Orchestra. I really want to see that."

"I guess that settles it," Maggie said. "We're going to hear some jazz tonight."

"That's fine with me," Katie spoke up.

Wynn said, "I'll pass on that, Mom. I think I'll change and go play some basketball. I saw an outside court that looks really nice. Just hang out a little and tour the ship."

"Well, okay, if that's what you want to do," Katie said.

Katie turned her attention to Sandra. "What are you going to do now, Sandra?"

"Oh, I think I'll just go back to the room and get some rest. Don't worry about me, Katie. You all just go out and have some fun, and I'll see you at breakfast tomorrow morning."

Katie replied, "Sandra, will you be okay in the room all by yourself?"

"Oh, I'll be fine, girl. I've got my bottle," Sandra said referring to a small bottle of gin that she smuggled onto the ship.

Ever since her experience the last time she was in Bermuda, Sandra had a change of spirit, but she still had her vices, and she always openly acknowledged it. Social drinking was one of them although never to excess.

Sandra continued, "Just don't be too loud when you come in. I'm sure I'll be fast asleep."

"Well, okay. If that's what you want to do," Katie replied.

§ § §

As everyone separated for their night's activities, Wynn went immediately to the top deck to witness the ship's departure from the port of New York. Together with a few other onlookers, everyone there had a clear view of the Manhattan skyline. As the ship started its journey even workers at the port waved their goodbyes to those on board as the cruisers gazed down over the railing. Slowly the vessel glided its way along the Hudson River passing well-known tourist attractions like the Empire State Building and eventually the Statue of Liberty. It was Wynn's first view of the part of the city that was on the other side of the river from his home back on Long Island.

As the cruise liner began its track across the Atlantic with the skyscrapers of Manhattan Island now getting smaller and smaller, Wynn realized that there was no turning back. The trip that he hesitated to take now gave him no options. He was on his way to Bermuda. He found contentment in the fact that soon he would be on the beach, and he loved everything the beach had to offer.

After Wynn witnessed the ship pulling off from the New York port headed toward Bermuda, he continued to relax on the top deck. He paused to view that massive Manhattan skyline, and imagined someone standing there in his arms, viewing the same. It would be the beginning of a grand experience. Now he was content as he stood there looking out toward the ocean beyond.

Figure 7: New York City Skyline at Twilight Viewed from the Ship

"For God so loved the world that He gave His only begotten Son, that whoever believes in Him should not perish but have everlasting life." (John 3:16)

The view of the city's skyline, while massive at first, gradually diminished as the ship moved out into the deep waters of the Atlantic Ocean. Soon there would be nothing but ocean—only water as far as the eye could see. The clear day had transitioned into twilight, so he decided to walk to the basketball court to get in a few hoops before total darkness of night set in, for he had other plans for the evening.

Several passengers lingered to see the vessel begin its sail from the port of New York. Wynn was one of the last to leave the ship's guard rail on the top deck that day. When he began his walk to the courts, he was ready to play ball. He had no misgivings about not joining his mother, the Mints, and the Manleys at the jazz concert. He loved the independence. After spending almost two hours playing ball, he became tired. He took a quick shower in a nearby refreshing room and then walked around to view some of the attractions on the ship.

Wynn eventually ventured to an area called the boardwalk, which featured games and a variety of boutiques like what you would find on a real boardwalk in Atlantic City. It brought to mind the time he and his mother visited a friend of hers there and made a visit to the famous Iron Landing, an amusement park on a long pier extending from the boardwalk out into the ocean. That's where he first was introduced to the beach, and it was love at first sight. The pier also offered a variety of small shops including a soda shop where mainly young people would hang out. After his beach experience, Wynn knew his life never would be quite the same again.

On his way to the soda shop onboard the ship, Wynn went by the lounge to check on his mother and everyone in the group one last time before the evening's festivities.

§ § §

Back in the lounge, Katie was anxious to have dinner. "Come on, everybody," she said. "Let's go and get something to eat. Then we can go our separate ways."

"That's sounds good, Katie. But let's go to our rooms and freshen up a bit first. Fred and I will be back in the room."

"Okay, Maggie," Katie replied.

Maggie continued, "Now, Gates, Courtney, and Katie, after we eat we can meet right back here before we go to the show."

But Katie responded, "Well, while you all go to your rooms, I'm going to walk around a little until you all return to this very spot—ready to eat.

Maggie replied, "Okay, Katie. We'll meet you here in a half hour and we all can eat."

Maggie turned to Wynn and Sandra, who would be left behind because they decided not to go to the show. "So you two are going to do your own thing tonight," she said. "Well, Wynn, you've already been to the basketball court. You did go there, didn't you?" she asked him directly.

He replied by saying simply, "Yeah, I had some fun."

Sandra replied to Maggie, "Yeah, me and Wynn will be fine."

"Well, we'll be listening to some good jazz in a little while. Yeah, I know you'll have fun, Wynn, since you have that room now to yourself. And don't worry; your mother will be with us, and she'll be fine," Maggie added as if he needed consoling.

But Wynn looked forward to being away from the group for the night.

Sandra repeated, "Yeah, Katie will be just fine."

"Yeah, Miss Sandra; my mom will be just fine, and, Miss Maggie, I hope you all have a good time!" Wynn replied.

Soon everyone disassembled. Wynn needed to return to his room after having explored various portions of the ship. He was glad it was now solely his room.

§ § §

The Manleys and the Mints spent a lot of the afternoon in their rooms resting; after a while they wanted go to the top deck to experience the open waters of the Atlantic. They had gotten the respite they needed before dinner and the jazz concert. Katie enjoying strolling the decks and seeing the sights on the ship.

Eventually everyone except Wynn and Sandra reunited to have the evening meal together. After eating a lavish meal, those who had decided to attend the concert made their way to where the event was to be held. Everyone was looking forward to having an exciting time there.

Once they arrived at the entrance to the main theater, Fred asked his wife, "Mag, did you anticipate such a long line?"

Maggie replied, "No, I didn't, Fred, but ask Gates about the crowds. He's the one who made the reservations and purchased the tickets."

Fred did what his wife had suggested.

"Well, Gates, what do you have to say about these long lines? I know you have connections. You can get us to the front of the line, can't you?" Fred asked.

Gates, who was with his wife Courtney, said forcefully to Fred in particular and to the others in general, "Come on, guys, I know it's going to be a little wait, but once we're in it'll be worth it. I guarantee that."

Katie said, "Now, Gates, how can you guarantee what you haven't seen?"

"That's just it, Katie. I have seen these guys perform before and they are really good. You'll see," Gates assured her.

After standing in line for about an hour, Maggie, Fred, Courtney, Gates, and Katie finally went inside. They were amazed at the size of the auditorium. It seemed too large for a cruise ship. Their seats ended up being on the floor section about twelve rows from the stage. The best part about that was they were on the first row of the second section with a wide space in front of their seats. There was a large space for dancing, and that's exactly what they did later during the concert.

"Wow, what great seats!" Courtney said to the others. Now they were ready to sit back and enjoy the show.

§ § §

While most members of the group attended the jazz concert, Wynn ended up at Max Soda shop on the boardwalk area of the ship. He saw a young lady sitting alone at one of the tables. As she sipped her beverage, Wynn went over and introduced himself.

"Hello there. My name is Wynn and I'm from New York. What's your name?" he asked confidently.

"My name is Jeanie," she said.

"I sense that you don't talk much, do you?" he said.

She turned her head, appearing to be too shy to answer.

Wynn added, "If I'm bothering you, I can leave."

"No, you're fine," she responded.

She thought to herself, *If only he knew what I was really thinking. He doesn't know that I think he's really, really fine, a fine and handsome guy! No Jeanie! Don't you dare say that to him!*

"You seem to do more thinking than talking," Wynn said. "Well, that's fine. I like quiet girls."

She smiled. "Well, I'm not that quiet," she said much more loudly.

"Okay, Okay, I get it! I believe you!" he said. "I don't want to get on your bad side. My goodness, we've just met," he said. "Mind if I join you?"

To that she simply responded, "No."

Wynn placed an order and began to talk some more to her. He wanted to learn as much as he could about Jeanie.

"Are you here with your folks?" Wynn asked.

"Yeah, they went to this jazz concert," she told him.

"Hey, that's where my folks went," he said.

"Really?"

"Yeah, they really love music," Wynn added. "I like a variety of music, even some country songs," he said.

"I think that's a little unusual, a city guy like you liking country," she said.

Without responding to that comment, Wynn made a proposition. "Listen, it's just gotten dark, and we could go on the top deck and just chill out there for a while. If nothing else, we could look at the stars and listen to the live band. I heard them earlier today and they're pretty good. They're playing around the swimming pool area. It's really a nice spot just to chill out."

"Yeah, I'd like that," Jeanie replied.

Jeanie soon finished her milkshake, and Wynn gobbled down some fries with his soda. They got ready to head to the top deck to listen to music and look at the stars. *How romantic would that be?* Wynn thought to himself. So off they went.

As they began their journey through the hallways and stairwells leading to the top deck, Wynn resisted the thought of taking her to perhaps an even better place, his cabin.

Little did Jeanie know that Wynn was a flirter. He liked being with girls at every opportunity, and he loved to be in serious relationships—in the plural. Much like his womanizing father even during his marriage, Wynn couldn't seem to keep away from the girls.

Katie always believed that Wynn took after his father and wanted more than his share of the opposite sex. That behavior led to her separation from her husband when she caught him in the arms of another woman. She eventually forgave him, and, with some professional therapy, they remained together for a while and pretended to have a good relationship. But things were never quite the same for the couple after that. She found out about his unfaithfulness with yet another woman not long after the first episode. With that, she decided to end the relationship for good, to leave him and take Wynn with her.

Katie always loved her son and would do anything for him, but earlier in his adolescence she observed that Wynn had taken on many of the traits of his father by having multiple relationships with different girls. He also inherited his father's temper.

On the ship Wynn found himself with yet another female companion. He met Jeanie on the first night of the cruise. That evening they were two of the few cruisers in this area of the ship. It was a little breezy. Fortunately, Wynn had brought his jacket and promptly offered it to Jeanie. They found a spot by themselves with only one other couple in their vicinity, but they were quite a distance from them. Wynn and Jeanie secured two beach chairs and some large towels from a nearby storage room, where an attendant helped them. Finally they just relaxed, sitting there listening to music, hearing the roar of the ocean, and gazing at the stars.

The slight wind and the vessel moving over the ocean waves caused a small roar as they journeyed towards their destination.

The crisp, cool air prompted Jeanie to say, "Ooh, I wish I had worn long sleeves; it's kinda cool out here! But you know what, Wynn? I feel that way only when the breeze kicks up."

Wynn replied, "Here, take my jacket. Don't worry; it's not sweaty because I didn't play basketball in it."

"Oh, I don't care, but what about you? Aren't you cool?" Jeanie asked.

"No. It's actually very nice out here. After all, it makes me warm just knowing you're warm!" Wynn said.

"Ooh, that's so sweet of you to say, Wynn!" she responded. As Wynn placed the coat over her shoulders, she was amazed at how large it was, but it provided the comfort that she hoped for. She really liked the jacket a lot, but he cared most about it.

"We can go inside in a little bit, but right now it's really nice out here, especially with something covering your arms, Jeanie," Wynn said. "Just to stay close to me," he said. So there they were, not much more than strangers yet in the arms of each other.

§ § §

"Tell me about your folks," Wynn said. "How did they decide to come on this trip?"

"Well, Wynn, it's like this: my natural father passed away a couple of months ago from a terminal illness."

Wynn interjected, "Oh no, Jeanie, I'm so sorry to hear that."

"Yeah, thanks," she responded. "Anyway, my mother met this guy not too long after my father's funeral. His name is David. But without getting into the details, he came on so strongly, Wynn, and I think my mother was so weak at the time that she fell for his advances. But, Wynn, he smokes and drinks a lot, and, to top that off, he sometimes uses vulgar language. I just don't think he's good for my mother, but she likes him. She may even love the guy. But I really don't think she's gotten over the loss of my father yet."

After giving Wynn that information, Jeanie started to get emotional and revealed something else to him.

She said, almost crying, "One day when we were alone, he even tried to hit on me. He got so close to me, Wynn, that I could smell his breath!"

"Oh no, Jeanie. He didn't!" Wynn said, his voice revealing his dismay. While Wynn responded almost in anger, inside himself he wanted to get close to her too. They snuggled against one another. Wanting to comfort Jeanie, he said, "Here; take this tissue and dry your eyes."

As Jeanie took and used what was offered, she said through sniffles, "I'm so glad that we met, Wynn."

"Yeah, I'm glad we met too," Wynn responded.

After some further discussion, Wynn said, "Let me ask you something. How long do you plan to be in Bermuda? You're staying here for a while, aren't you?"

"Yes, we're staying for three days, and we're leaving here on Sunday," she answered.

"Hey, let me guess. Would you happen to be returning on the 4:00 cruise back to New York?" he asked.

"Why, yes, that's when we're going back," Jeanie answered.

"Well, we're going back on that cruise liner too, so we'll be able to see each other again while going back to New York!" he said rather enthusiastically.

She replied, "I'm so glad, Wynn. I guess we'll be seeing a lot of each other over the next few days," she gladly said.

"Well, I sure look forward to that!" he responded.

After about another hour of chatter, Wynn said, "It's been so nice up here with you. I guess it's about time to leave. Let me walk you back to your cabin, and I can continue to my room. I really need to take a shower. I washed up a little bit after I stopped playing ball, but I really need to get back and freshen up more back in my room."

As Wynn and Jeanie journeyed back to her room, they stopped to take a look at a magnificent sunset – yes, Jeanie was in the arms of a guy she was growing to like very much. Wynn immediately thought about standing at that very spot earlier, viewing the massive Manhattan skyline at the beginning of twilight, only wishing that Jeanie was with him. But she *was* with him now, and that was good enough.

Soon they continued their walk to her living quarters. Jeanie was intrigued with what Wynn last told her about being alone in his cabin. So she asked simply but with great curiosity, "Wynn, do you have your own room?"

Wynn responded, "Yeah, I was rooming with my mother, but she decided to move in with a friend of hers who came with us on this trip. Yeah, her friend was all alone, so she decided to move in with her and left me in the room all by myself."

"Wow," Jeanie responded. "It must really be nice having your own room on the ship."

Wynn replied, "Yeah, maybe we can go there tomorrow night, our last night on this ship."

"Yeah, I'd like that, I think," Jeanie said with her voice hesitating as she considered what her folks would think about her being alone with a boy in a room on the ship. But she held her feelings to herself. She said, "Okay, I guess I should be going back too. I'm staying with my folks, and I want to be in the room when they return from that concert."

Wynn thought that it was interesting that a teenage girl was staying in the same room as her mother and boyfriend, especially since the cabins were not that large. That was just too close a physical living arrangement in Wynn's estimation. He couldn't help thinking about what Jeanie had said about her mother's friend making a pass at her.

Wynn and Jeanie were on their way back to their rooms when they saw a small bench. Wynn said, "Let's sit here for a while before you go in for the night."

Just before saying goodnight to her, he asked Jeanie a final question about her folks' lodgings while in Bermuda. "So, are you all staying at the resort? That's where we're staying," he added.

She replied in a somewhat dejected fashion, "No, Wynn. We're not staying there or at any other resort on the beach. We're at a hotel away from the oceanfront near downtown Bermuda. That's all mother could afford. Well, at least I'll have my own bed."

Wynn interjected, "Your own bed? Well, where are you sleeping now?"

Jeanie was somewhat embarrassed to answer, but she tried anyway. She said, "Well, we were able to get a very nice suite with a pull-out sofa. I guess you might call it a cot. It's kinda like an extension of the bed that they are sleeping on, and I'm sleeping on it. Anyway, we decided to stay in the room before venturing out earlier in the day, and we took a nap. So that's our sleeping arrangement right now."

Jeanie continued to give more details about her accommodations. "But, Wynn, I know it was only in the afternoon, but it was so dark in there even in broad daylight. And I can't imagine being in there for the time that we're on this cruise. I mean today I could hear everything they were doing. It was so embarrassing for me."

After hearing what Jeanie had to say, Wynn sounded somewhat stunned as he responded, "Wait a minute. Are you saying you're now sleeping in the same cabin as where your folks are? Your mother and her boyfriend?"

Jeanie replied back to him, "Why, yeah, that's right. Like I said, it's kind of like an extension of the bed they're sleeping on."

"What?" Wynn asked. "An extension? Why, it's almost like you're sleeping in the same bed with 'em, for heaven's sake!" he added. Wynn tried to provide her with some comfort when he said, "Well, at least you'll be there for only one more night."

"Yeah, you're right, Wynn. I think I can put up with it until we get to Bermuda," she told him, trying to assure him that she was okay with the temporary arrangement.

Wynn thought to himself about Jeanie's living quarters, *how in the world can she sleep in the same room with 'em?*

Before he could respond to the last thing that she had told him, Jeanie repeated her sentiments from earlier. "I hope we'll be able to see each other over the next few days Wynn. You're kinda' fun to be with," Jeanie confessed to her new friend.

"Yeah, I'm sure we'll see each other," Wynn said. A momentary thought came to his mind. *I can't wait to take advantage of that room I have all to myself tomorrow night before we leave the ship! Just imagine Jeanie and me alone there,* he pondered.

Wynn and Jeanie got up from the bench, and he gave her a big hug as they parted ways at the door of her folks' cabin. He had gotten her cabin number earlier so they would be in constant contact with one another the next day. He anticipated being with her again the following evening, the last night of the cruise to Bermuda.

§ § §

The next morning everyone in Maggie's group woke up to a bright clear day. Only Sandra was well rested because, unlike the others, she stayed in her room and drank the alcoholic beverage she had managed to slip on board. She got up and went to the top deck, where Wynn had spent time a day earlier to witness the ship's departure from the New York port.

The cool, moist but clear early summer air later felt wonderful as she witnessed the sun rising like a huge orange ball. It steadily ascended above the ocean's horizon, casting a reflection on the waters as it became smaller and smaller with its ascension in the morning sky. Sandra stood there, meditating and anxiously anticipating her reunion with Erin the next day in Bermuda. She fantasized how, like that rising sun, the fortunes in her love life would also rise. She thought about how it would be, standing on a cruise ship with the man of her dreams, viewing the sun rising above the horizon as she now witnessed. In her spiritual renewal, she no longer desired to be in the arms of a married man like Fred, but the desire of being with someone never left her.

Figure 8: Sunrise Over the Ocean Seen from the Ship

"Through the tender mercy of our God, With which the Dayspring from on high has visited us; To give light to those who sit in darkness, and the shadow of death. To guide our feet into the way of peace." (Luke 1:78,79)

Fred and Maggie remained in their cabin that morning, where he started to work on the manuscript of the book he was writing.

Gates, Courtney, Fred, and Maggie were so very tired after their night at the concert that they slept well into the late morning.

When Katie came into the room after the concert, she found her new roommate fast asleep. The next morning Katie remained in slumber as Sandra got up and started stirring around the small cabin. The noise was enough to wake Katie from a sound sleep.

Still tired from a night of dancing at the concert, she asked Sandra, "Are you still planning to jog around the ship like you said you would do yesterday?"

"Yeah, I'll be ready in a few minutes. But let me warn you, I like to move at a good pace. And I know that you're tired from last night. I didn't even hear you get into bed. So do you think you can keep up with me?"

"Oh yeah, girl, I can keep up," Katie replied. "You know, I might just walk faster than you," she added, becoming more energetic and alert as she joked with Sandra.

Katie was determined to fight the fatigue that was brought on by a night of fun at the concert.

"Do you know, Sandra, that I ran track in high school? So I think I can hold my own."

"Well, I guess you can," Sandra replied, surprised that she had a history in organized track and field. Sandra continued, "Anyway, like I said, I'll be ready in a few minutes. Let me go and put on some sweatpants and a top."

"Okay, Sandra, I'll do the same, and I'll be ready in ten minutes," Katie said.

Sandra, who was well rested because she stayed in her room the prior evening, was ready to run with Katie as they had discussed a day ago. Once on the track that encircled the ship, they walked a little and ran a little.

They did the walk/run routine for a good hour and then returned to the room. That's when Sandra said to Katie, "I'm surprised that you were able to keep up with me."

Katie replied, "Like I said, I ran track in high school. But it was a little tiring, I must admit, because I stayed up so late last night enjoying the show. It probably was easier for you since you stayed in last night."

"Yeah, girl, I was well rested this morning and I'm still rested now. I'll just be glad when we get to Bermuda," Sandra replied.

Katie added, "Well, we both got in a nice workout on the track this morning."

"Well, like I said, I'll be glad when we get to Bermuda Katie."

Katie nodded her head in agreement and said, "Yeah, me too."

Katie really looked forward to meeting Sandra's friend Erin. Sandra had talked about her so much, and it was all good. With their morning exercise behind them, they began to freshen up and dress to start the rest of their day, beginning with breakfast at a restaurant where everyone had agreed to meet.

§ § §

Courtney and Gates and Maggie and Fred rose late and had coffee in their cabins. After dressing, the couples met each other at the café, Boarders. Before too long, everyone finally came together for lunch there on the boardwalk part of the ship.

Wynn already had met Jeanie earlier in the morning for breakfast at one of the smaller eateries called the Joint. It was the ship's version of a waffle house and served only breakfast food.

After that early breakfast, Jeanie returned to her folks' cabin, and Wynn prepared to meet the other members of his group for lunch. Once everyone arrived at Boarders, Sandra asked, "How was the concert last night?"

Maggie responded, "It was grand. The music was fantastic, and the best thing was that we got a chance to dance, and, girl, we just danced the night away!" Maggie said joyfully.

"Amen to that," Courtney added.

"Well, that's great," Sandra replied.

Then Maggie asked, "How was your evening, Sandra? You stayed in your room, didn't you? I mean you didn't slip out and go anywhere, did you? Am I right about that?"

"Yes, Maggie, you're right. I stayed in my room, and I enjoyed every minute of it. Yeah, I really appreciated the rest," Sandra said with a certain degree of conviction. Sandra continued, "I'm sure I'll go out more once we get to Bermuda."

Katie turned to Wynn and asked, "How was your evening, son?"

"Oh, it was fine, Mom. I met this nice young lady – and we hit it off immediately – she's really a nice girl," he said.

"I hope you behaved yourself," she said.

"Wynn replied with disdain, "Oh, Mom, don't start gettin' personal in my business."

"Okay, Okay, Wynn, I'll try to be objective about it," Katie said reacting to her son's apparent displeasure at her comments. She continued, "I know you'll treat the young lady right—just like a lady."

"Yeah, Mom, that's how I intend to treat her, just like a lady," Wynn said. He didn't mention to his mother that they had met earlier in the morning for breakfast.

With that, Katie stopped the inquiry, knowing that in the past she had little to no influence on the girls that he went out with. She only hoped that it would be different with Jeanie. She did want to meet her.

As everyone entered Boarders, they were overwhelmed by all the food selections. There were different meats, pasta, and vegetables and a separate section for desserts. There also was an area with beverages of all kinds. Most of the non-drink items had been already prepared and placed in warming trays for people to view and make their selections. The eatery also had chefs stationed at certain locations to prepare specific entrees to order.

As Maggie's group stood at the entrance to the restaurant, Fred said, "Hey, let me go over there and claim three tables so that all of us can sit together." Fred made sure the tables were available and then led the group over after entering the cafeteria style eatery. Eventually everyone took their seats and partook of a scrumptious meal and chatted among themselves while gazing out huge windows at the rolling waves of the sea.

§ § §

Once everyone finished their lunch, they scattered. They were eager to start preparing to get off the cruise liner first thing in the morning. Everyone including Wynn spent the remainder of the afternoon and evening getting ready for their departure from the ship the next day.

Wynn looked forward to meeting Jeanie again later when she would visit his cabin for the first time.

The early afternoon of the last full day of the cruise to Bermuda was like the previous ones, warm, sunny, and breezy. Without warning, over the loudspeaker an announcement was made about the possibility of inclement weather over the next several days. They were predicting the possibility of a hurricane, which was the last thing anyone on this trip wanted to hear. But the forecast still called for sunny conditions over the next several days, the time in which the group would be in Bermuda. The forecast did indicate that if the system got more intense, it would definitely affect Bermuda and the surrounding area by the time the group would be ready to depart the island in about four days. For now the announcement was just a precautionary measure to let everyone know the possibilities.

Maggie refused to let the forecast dampen the plans of her and the group. She still looked forward to having a great time.

Everyone was preparing for departure from the ship the next day. But Wynn had only one thing on his mind, Jeanie. She too looked forward to their meeting and going to his cabin before the end of the evening.

Jeanie's mother Sheri continued to obsess over her friend David and mixed their preparation to depart the ship with last-minute recreational activities that may have been provided on the last night of the cruise to Bermuda.

Jeanie didn't have a problem explaining to her mother how she would be spending the evening. Sheri and David pretty much let her have her own way and do whatever she wanted with whom she wanted to do it. Jeanie's mother and friend were too busy trying to squeeze every bit of pleasure they could from what the ship had to offer. And even on this last night of the cruise, there were still plenty of things to take advantage of on board.

Wynn wanted the pleasure of being with Jeanie alone. She had already packed her belongings earlier in the day. Jeanie was alone in her cabin while Sheri and David were out having a good time. But Wynn wanted to be with her alone in his cabin. He suspected that Jeanie's folks might return at any time. Earlier when they met for breakfast, Jeanie gave Wynn a time to come by her cabin to pick her up when her folks were likely not to be there. Jeanie knew that Sheri had made reservations for an event that was supposed to start at 4:00 in the afternoon, and that's when she asked Wynn to pick her up. Once they departed from each other at breakfast, it would be a long day before they would come together again.

The time finally came when Jeanie expected Wynn to come by her cabin. It was a few minutes after the 4:00 hour when he knocked on the door; she quickly let him in. They greeted one another with great anticipation.

"Hello, Jeanie. You look so pretty," Wynn said. "I really like the pantsuit you have on. It looks as though it was made for you."

"Aw, Wynn, you say the nicest things. I've had this outfit ever since junior high school. I was much larger than my classmates at that time but haven't grown a lot since."

Jeanie asked, "Do you want something to drink?"

"No, I'm good," he answered. "You know, you're making me feel just like I'm at home."

Jeanie said, "You know I'm really a homebody."

"Well, I hope it's good, me being here," Wynn told Jeanie.

She replied, "You're good. It's only late at night and early in the morning when my folks are here. Yeah, they're only here when they go to bed and that's when it really gets congested in here—when they're in the cabin with me, I mean. So they won't be here until much later," she told him.

Jeanie continued, "But do you know what, Wynn? I'm so glad they're not here much because it means that I won't have to see him, David I mean. I just don't like the way he looks at me, Wynn; it seems as though he could tear into me at any moment. It's pretty scary. Sorry, Wynn, for placing all this on you. I guess you're trying to figure out what I'm talking about," she said.

"Oh no. I know exactly what you're talking about, Jeanie. You're in an unfortunate situation," Wynn added. "You're not very comfortable around him at all, are you? David, I mean."

"No, Wynn, not comfortable at all," Jeanie responded, almost in tears. "Especially at night when I have to sleep on that extension from their bed that I was telling you about—and I can hear *everything*. It's so gross having to sleep in the same room as your folks. Anyway I don't want to bore you with my problems."

While trying his best to console Jeanie, Wynn offered a chance for her family to be with his group during their stay in Bermuda.

"You know, Jeanie, because of the living arrangement you told me about, not being on the beach and all, you and your folks can be with us during our stay in Bermuda. We have a nice place on the beach. It's a resort that a friend of my mother knows about through another friend. Well, it's a little complicated, but you will get to know all of them. Just ask your folks if they would agree to that, and I'll mention it to my people too. But I'm sure my family and friends would be receptive to the idea."

"Wynn, that would be great! I'll do that. I'll mention that to my mother and David," Jeanie assured him.

Wynn tried to turn the discussion to something more positive than Jeanie's living arrangement.

"Hey, Jeanie, let's go out on the top deck again. I really enjoyed it when we were there last night."

"Okay, could you step into the bathroom until I put something on that's more casual?" she asked.

"Sure, I'll do better than that. I'll wait outside for you—right outside in the hallway. I'll be sitting on that bench."

"Cool, I'll be right out," she said.

§ § §

When she finished changing, Jeanie came outside her cabin wearing shorts and a loose top; she found Wynn and they were off to the top of the deck. As they journeyed there, they did a lot of sightseeing, observing the various venues the ship had to offer. They passed a casino and what appeared to be two expensive looking restaurants decorated with white tablecloths and lit candles with soft music playing.

Once they got to their destination on the open deck, they picked up towels and found some beach chairs. Like the previous day, they just lay there enjoying the scene before them—ocean all around and other cruisers in their swim attire lazing nearby or walking past without any hurry. The sound of music played by a band on a small stage near the pool added to the atmosphere.

After staying there for a while, Wynn said to Jeanie, "You know, I'm a little hungry. I don't know about you, but I haven't eaten since our group ate at Boarders."

Jeanie responded, "Yeah, I went with mom and David to lunch but didn't eat much. Yeah, let's go. I'm ready to eat too."

So they gathered their belongings and proceeded to a sandwich shop to grab a bite. While there they chatted about various things. After finishing their meal, they walked to his cabin.

Soon night fell. Since being with Jeanie over the course of his time on the cruise, his heart had softened a lot toward her. Usually the flirtatious son that his mother knew, he had somehow been transformed from someone who only wanted to be intimate with Jeanie into someone who genuinely liked her. Perhaps it was because of the family history that she described to him. But whatever the case, his thoughts of Jeanie being just another girl for him to take advantage of were a distant memory. This was true even if his mother had not been convinced.

As they walked to his cabin, they passed the casino again. Jeanie blurted out, "Oh, Wynn, this is another thing David does." She pointed towards the casino. "He loves to play the slot machines. I know my mother never did that before she met him. He's definitely changed her," she said.

"Well, I've never been into gambling," Wynn replied.

After a long, slow walk, Wynn and Jeanie finally got to his cabin. When they had arrived and entered, she was amazed at how small it was. They hopped onto the bed and just sat there continuing to talk about all sorts of things.

"Wynn, I'm not surprised that your mother wanted to move out of this cabin," Jeanie said. "It would have been so cramped with you and your mother sleeping so close to one another."

"Yeah, it would have been very cramped with her in the room. But being here alone is very nice, especially being here alone with you."

"Oh, Wynn, you say the nicest things."

After those complimentary comments, Wynn changed the subject. "Listen, Jeanie, I want to confess something to you. I've seen plenty of girls, but you're different. I have to admit that at first I wanted to get you into my room and have sex with you to be blunt about it. But for some reason, being the nice girl that you are, I don't have those feelings anymore," he told her almost at the point of crying. "Do you know what I mean?" he asked.

Jeanie answered him, "Oh, Wynn, I really appreciate your honesty, being so blunt. You know that's very unusual. A lot of guys wouldn't have the courage to admit such a thing. But you know what? I think I do know what you mean, because I've had some of the same thoughts. You know, Wynn, we're both young and human with natural desires of affection, and there's nothing wrong with that. It just has to be under control. And, fortunately, I think you're in the process of getting that part of your life under control, and I guess, based on what you're saying, I've had some part in your doing that."

Jeanie continued, "And you know what, Wynn? Somehow because of your demeanor, I knew you weren't that kind of guy to take advantage of girls—at least girls who respected themselves and who didn't desire to be in the arms of just any guy. Now let me return the question, Wynn. Do you understand what *I'm* trying to say?"

He responded, "I think so, Jeanie. But our discussion has turned much too technical. Let's just enjoy the evening."

Jeanie replied, "That sounds good to me!"

Jeanie wanted to get something else out in the open with Wynn before they totally left their intimate discussion. They continued sitting on his bed with their backs against the wall.

At last she said, "Now, Wynn, I don't pretend to know all the answers about confronting life's many issues, but there's this one thing that has been bugging me lately, and it has to do with David. And I've had my share of issues since he moved into our lives—I mean me and my mother's life. I was brought up in church and I believe that has formed a foundation for my life up to this point."

"Okay, that's interesting," Wynn interjected before Jeanie had a chance to complete her point. He continued, "My mother attends church a lot too, and I think she's developed some of those same thoughts that you've just mentioned about church, and I have to admit to you, Jeanie, I'm still learning about all that. But it's difficult for me to accept some of these church ideas, especially after being in school. There are just so many things you have to deal with there, including me having to make a decision about college or just getting a job some place," he told her.

Wynn continued, "You know, Jeanie, my mom said that her friend, the one that she's moved in with on this cruise, met a person in Bermuda that had a great effect on her life. I believe her name is Erin. Well, I can't wait to find out who this person is. And maybe she can help the both of us with the challenges we have too," Wynn added.

Jeanie responded, "That's interesting, Wynn. Like I told you before, I'll mention what you said about my family getting together with your group and see what they say. But I believe they'll go for it. Oh, Wynn, I can't wait to get to Bermuda. I'm really excited about it."

After that Wynn walked Jeanie back to her cabin where she would continue to pack her things for disembarking the ship in the morning with her folks. Wynn came back to his room and finished packing.

The next morning Wynn met with other members of his group. Everyone followed protocol in the disembarkation process. Soon they were off the ship and in a ground transportation area waiting for their luggage. In the case of Maggie's group, Erin would be there to pick everyone up; she had made arrangements to transport the group and their belongings to her resort in Bermuda. So the time had finally come when everyone would meet Sandra's friend Erin.

REFERENCE

"Ask, and it will be given to you; seek, and you will find; knock, and it will be open to you. For everyone who asks receives and he who seeks find and to him who knocks, it will be opened." (Matthew 7:7-8)

4. BERMUDA — THE FIRST DAY AND NIGHT

The cruise ship approached the port of Bermuda at about 6:00 in the morning. Because of all the last-minute packing late into the previous night, Wynn was the only member of Maggie's group who rose early to experience the cruise liner's entry into the harbor. After getting out of bed, he threw on something light and proceeded up to the top deck.

Looking out over the ship's railing, he said, "Whew!!! It sure is cool out here this morning." But he withstood the chilling temperatures and witnessed the first sight of land in two days. As they approached the island, Wynn was amazed at all the greenery of Bermuda.

Back in Maggie and Fred's cabin, there was a buzz of activity. They too had risen early but had decided to use their time to make last-minute preparations for leaving the ship. They had completed their packing the night before and had placed everything beside the cabin door, where it was picked up by ship personnel and taken off the cruise liner to a docking area. It remained there until cruisers were led off the ship and taken to retrieve their belongings.

Everyone eventually arrived in the docking area where long lines of people waited to claim their luggage. While standing in one of these with other cruisers, Maggie saw two other members of the group.

"Hey, Courtney. Hey, Gates," she yelled. "I guess you two completed your packing okay."

With everyone nearby staring, Courtney called, "Hey, Maggie, and hey to you too, Fred."

Courtney continued to holler back at Maggie, making some around them a bit uncomfortable. "Yeah, it was something getting everything prepared to leave this ship. But listen, Maggie, I've enjoyed every minute of being on this cruise."

"Yeah, girl, it's been a blast, especially the first night when we went to that concert. I think that I'm still tired from all that dancing we did. Yeah, all of us had a good time there," Maggie continued in a loud voice that carried over the distance between them and the other cruisers who stood nearby.

A lady who was not a part of Maggie's group called out to both Maggie and Courtney, "I know what you two mean, because my husband and I went to that concert too, and we loved it! We didn't do any dancing though!" she added.

With those comments everyone in the vicinity just burst out laughing. All the commotion caused by Maggie and Courtney's shouted conversation lessened some of the frustration of those who were in line waiting to retrieve their belongings.

Katie, her son Wynn, and her cabin mate Sandra were also in one of the departure lines, but neither Maggie nor Courtney could spot them.

Soon all members of Maggie's group would be together again along with their luggage. Everyone looked forward to meeting Sandra's friend Erin, who would be waiting for them in a vehicle pickup area with a large shuttle that would take everyone to her resort. She would be their host for the next several days. Everyone anticipated an exciting vacation in Bermuda.

§ § §

After everybody retrieved their luggage, they stood together on the curbside waiting for Erin to arrive.

Maggie, who was chatting with Sandra, mentioned to her, "Sandra, I never imagined Bermuda being this beautiful. It actually reminds me of when I first went to Hawaii with John."

After a brief pause, Sandra noticed that Maggie had tears welling in her eyes. But she quickly composed herself and continued the conversation.

"Sorry, Sandra. I still get a little emotional when I think about it—that is, how John and I first visited Hawaii and how it all turned out when he confronted Fred. Yeah, it was the best and the worst of times. But thinking of the better aspects of that trip, I was mesmerized by all the greenery there at the Village Hotel where we stayed so long ago. Well, that was only a poor imitation of this. I mean, *this* is the real thing. Look at those birds over there, and I think that some of them are flamingos just like the ones I saw at the hotel in Hawaii."

During Maggie's positive, sometimes even emotional recollection of her time in Hawaii, Fred interjected, "Mag, I'm glad you remember those good times because for me things weren't so good at all when I met your husband. I guess we both were very adventurous."

Trying to be more uplifting, Sandra said, "Come on now; let's bring some positive excitement in here. We're in Bermuda. And like you said, Maggie, this is the real thing. Everything is so natural here."

Sandra knew what it meant to be here, to experience not only the natural beauty of the place but also its spiritual aspects, stemming from her experience with Erin.

Soon everyone saw the resort shuttle approaching, and their excitement was immediately enhanced. When their transport arrived, Erin was anxious to step out and meet everyone. As she exited the vehicle, smiling from ear to ear, she looked at everyone and said, "Hello, everybody. I'm Erin and it's so nice to finally see all of you. I've been looking forward to this moment ever since I was told that you all were coming."

Soon Erin was surrounded by everyone in Maggie's group. She said, "I hope you all had a pleasant trip. I'm anxious to get to talk with all of you."

Then Erin glanced at Sandra and suddenly became emotional. She said, "Oh, Sandra, I've looked forward to seeing you again somehow ever since you left this place. You know how much it means to me to see you."

Sandra responded, "Erin, believe me I'm as excited as you are, and I think you know why. But, listen, we owe all of this to Maggie and her close friend Gates. They're the reasons we're here in the first place."

When Sandra mentioned Maggie, Erin became emotional again.

"Oh, Maggie" she exclaimed. "I've heard so much about you from Sandra, and it's so nice to finally meet you. But it feels as though I already know you from our phone conversations."

Maggie, who was able to contain her emotions, just smiled and said, "Erin, Bermuda is everything Sandra said it would be. And it's great to finally meet you in person. But, listen, I know you have a job to do. And that is to get all of us down to the resort."

"Oh, Maggie, Sandra, and all of you, we're going to have such a good time this week! But, hey, we have to get there first. So I'm asking you start boarding, and your luggage will be placed in the storage compartment of the vehicle by our driver."

After an emotional introduction, everyone was ready to have their luggage loaded and taken with them to Erin's resort, the Golden

Retreat, for four days of fun. It was the same resort Sandra had visited when she was in Bermuda, but, because of some managerial decisions, the name was changed from when Sandra was last there.

Gates and Courtney were the first ones to board, taking their seats directly behind the driver. The other members of the group found their spots. All were eager to sightsee as they took the ten-mile ride from the Bermuda port to the resort. Soon they would arrive at the Golden Retreat, where they would take their luggage and get situated in their rooms.

Maggie rekindled Sandra's memory of all the positive things she told her about the experience she had in Bermuda. Those memories led Sandra to share those experiences, but she wanted Erin to help her.

"Erin," Sandra called passionately, "Come on over here and tell Maggie what it means to absorb everything that Bermuda has to offer." She continued, "All of the nature here has a freeing effect; at least it did for me. When I was here last, I had the chance to escape the city environment and appreciate nature a lot more. And believe you me, I really needed it, when you consider how sick I was and the injuries I received from my car accident. Erin can tell you about it."

Sandra was intent on having Maggie receive information about this tropical paradise firsthand from Erin. "Go ahead, Erin," she said. "Tell Maggie some of the things you know about Bermuda."

"I'm going to talk to Maggie first thing in the morning before breakfast," Erin replied. "That's when we can have some quality time, and I can give her more of the details."

"That sounds good, Erin," Sandra replied to her idea.

Erin continued, "And before we do that, Sandra, you're going to help me prepare food for everybody, and Maggie can help too. Is that okay, Maggie?" Erin asked.

"Well, sure I'll help you, Erin. What can I say? You're hosting us. And I'm sure you'll be a very good host," Maggie responded as though she had no choice in the matter.

Erin said, "Well, yes, I do want you to help me. But don't worry. I won't work you too hard. And, besides, I'm sure you'll learn some great dishes you can take back home. But mainly I'll plan to fill you in about a lot of details concerning this place. I think you'll be surprised."

Sandra interjected, "Now wait a minute, Erin, I want to know some of those things too. Don't leave me out!"

Erin replied, "Well, Sandra, you'll be with us, but you know a lot already. Anyway whether you're with us or not, I'm sure Maggie will fill you in about anything you may miss. Remember how you informed Maggie's mother, Mensie, about your stay here? And you probably told Maggie a lot directly yourself."

Turning away from Sandra for the moment, Erin continued, "I know that you are the matriarch of this group, Maggie. And …."

Before Erin could finish, Maggie interrupted. "Okay, Erin. But don't call me a matriarch because that sounds so *old*." She quickly added, "I'm sorry. You know I'm kidding you, I hope."

Erin said, "Okay, Maggie, I hear what you're saying." She continued, "Well, Maggie and Sandra, let me go and start some of the prep for that breakfast I was just talking about. But you two go ahead and continue talking all you want to each other, and I'll see you a little later this evening. But remember, all of you have your rooms assigned, and, if you have any problems or concerns, just give me a yell."

Maggie replied, "Erin, you just go and do what you need to do, and me and Sandra will be fine."

When Erin had gone to the kitchen, Sandra shared more with Maggie about how her time in Bermuda helped her. She made a comment about nature that had a spiritual tone to it. "Girl, this place is like heaven to me," Sandra said. "After all, God placed Adam and Eve in a garden, and obviously it was all natural—that is until Adam messed things up."

Fred spoke up and said, "Now wait a minute, Sandra. He ate the forbidden fruit only because Eve told him too."

Sandra replied, "Well, you know, Fred, the man is the head of the house, so he shouldn't have done what Eve told him to do, knowing that it was something God wanted them both to avoid."

Fred retorted, "Yeah, I understand that, and the scripture also says that women should be submissive to their husbands since God made man the head."

With that last comment by Fred, Maggie spoke up. "Now listen, you two. We're here to have a good time, not to debate scripture." Going against what she had just said, Maggie reminded Fred, "But you do know, honey, that last scripture you quoted means that as long as the husband is doing what the wife wants him to do, she's supposed to submit! And that's the difference, man!" she scolded him.

Fred retorted, "Oh, yeah? Well, you do know that's what got Adam in trouble in the first place, doing what she told him to do."

Maggie replied, "Well, Fred, you got me there!"

Fred said to his wife, "Okay, Mag; I thought you wanted us to move on from this debate."

Maggie replied, "Fred, you do know in reality there's no debate to what I said!"

Sandra said softly, "Amen to that!"

Once that debate ended, Maggie continued, "Anyway, I'm looking forward to all that this place has to offer over the next few days. Sandra, maybe we can take advantage of some of the experience you've had here. Yeah, the more I think about it, the more I believe that all of us can take advantage of your knowledge of this place."

Sandra responded, "Yeah, Maggie, but it's not me that you'll be learning a lot about Bermuda from; it's Erin, who has lived here for a while. And, Maggie, I guess the discussion between me and your husband about that forbidden fruit did get a little heated. But, Fred, I meant nothing by it," she added, trying to patch things up.

Fred said, "Aw, don't worry about it. I just pray that all of us get something from being here."

Erin, who overheard all the emotion that both Maggie and her friend Sandra had about the physical setting of the island and not forgetting about the spiritual aspects that it could provide, looked forward to providing whatever influence she could make on her guests over the next few days.

After just a little while, Erin returned from the kitchen area to the lobby where she had spoken to Maggie and Sandra earlier. She said addressing the both of them, "Hey, Sandra, I'll be getting together with everyone and giving information about Bermuda, but you are familiar with Bermuda too, having been here before. I want you to make sure that Maggie and all of her friends have the time of their lives while they're here."

Erin noticed some people in the group with whom she had not spoken, and she asked, "And who is this nice-looking couple here?" She looked directly at Gates and Courtney.

Gates said, "Hello, Erin. This is my wife Courtney, and I'm Gates. We've heard a lot about you, and it's been all good."

"Well, that's good to know," Erin replied.

Gates continued, "Bermuda is all I thought it would be—at least from what I've been able to research—and, believe me, I did a lot of research on the place, and I was impressed. Having finally arrived, I'm impressed with what I'm seeing so far."

"Well, Gates, and you too, Courtney, you're in for some big surprises. Some pleasant surprises, I might add," Erin told them.

As Erin made her way around to see all of Maggie's friends, she finally came to Wynn and his mother Katie.

"And who do we have here?" she asked.

Katie responded, "I'm Katie and this is my son Wynn. It's so nice to meet you. We're looking forward to being here over the next few days."

Erin said, "Great to have you both here. I know it'll be only four days—actually only three days since you're scheduled to leave on the fourth—but we're going to make the most of it, I'm sure," she said reassuring the entire group.

Erin returned her attention to Maggie and said, "You have a nice group here."

Maggie agreed. "Well, Erin, it's all because of Gates over there. He's the reason we're all here because of a promotion from his company."

Erin said to Gates, "Well, thank you, sir."

Maggie added, "Oh, yeah, another thing I want to tell you about… There's this couple that came down with us on the cruise, and they're staying at a cheap hotel near downtown Bermuda. Wynn over there—he can tell you about it. He met this girl who is the daughter of this couple, and he took it upon himself to invite them all to be with us over here at the resort. By the way, Wynn's new friend's name is Jeanie.

"I know it's complicated, Erin, but you'll get a chance to talk to Wynn and his friend Jeanie about it, I'm sure. I'd especially like for you to meet Jeanie's parents. Well, it's actually her mother Sheri and Sheri's friend David. I think it'd be good to have Jeanie and her folks join us. I hope that's okay," Maggie said.

Erin replied, "Sure. I think that would be great."

Despite Erin's favorable response, she perceived uncertainty in Maggie, which prompted Erin to say, "You seem hesitant about asking to have someone else join us, Maggie, but, believe me, it's all right. I believe the more the merrier. I'm sure they'll be fine. It's true that the more people you have the more complicated things can get because of everyone's different personalities. But I think it should be interesting. This place needs to be livened up a bit," Erin said.

"Anyway, I'm looking forward to meeting them," Erin added. "There's plenty of room here at the resort, and I'd be more than happy to accommodate them. You tell them that, or at least let your friend's son know so he can tell his friend, their daughter, it'd be just fine for them to join us. I'll leave all that up to you to sort out," Erin said to Maggie. She added, "Downtown is no place for tourists. Not only is there nothing there to speak of, at least for a tourist, but it's so much better here on the beach. They'll see, Jeanie's folks, I mean. And I'll tell you another thing: it's a lot safer here too."

Erin was hopeful that Jeanie's folks would join them. She said, "Anyway, I hope that Jeanie, her mom and mother's friend decide to come be with us. Like I said, the more the merrier."

Maggie was encouraged by what Erin had said as were Katie and Wynn, who overheard the conversation while standing at a distance talking to each other.

Katie whispered to her son, "Did you hear that, Wynn? Erin just welcomed Jeanie and her folks to join us at the resort—yeah, to be with us!"

Wynn replied, "That's really great."

Katie added, "Okay! Since you like their daughter, I imagine you're really looking forward to them agreeing to be with us."

Wynn responded, "Yes, Mom, I am looking forward to being with her, and I'm sure her folks will fit in with us too. I'll be sure to call Jeanie to let her know that all of them are welcome here."

Wynn walked over to tell Erin that he and his mother overheard her conversation with Maggie.

"Ms. Erin, I heard you all talking, so let me say that I'll contact my friend about them joining us. I'll let Jeanie bring it up to them."

Erin replied, "Well, I'm glad to hear that. I hope they will agree."

Erin said more directly to everybody assembled, "Well, I think things are pretty much set for us to have a grand weekend." She added, "Listen, everyone, dinner will be served tonight in the main dining area. It's not the most sophisticated place of dining that we have, but it will serve its purpose. And that purpose is to have all the food you can eat! After that, everyone can come to a large lounging area to talk and relax."

Erin added, "And, Wynn, make sure you tell this to your friend Jeanie so she can inform her folks. We all are looking forward to meeting them."

Wynn nodded to confirm what his mother had told him already.

Erin shouted to the rest of the group, "Now, is everybody ready to have a good time here the rest of the week?"

Maggie spoke up in response. "That sounds great, Erin. Praise the Lord! Can't wait! And I'm sure everyone here feels the same way."

§ § §

Soon everyone started to separate, and Erin and Sandra ended up in a corner of the lounge.

"Erin," Sandra said. "It's so nice to be here again with you."

Ignoring her comment, Erin simply said, "Let's go out and sit on those patio chairs; as you probably remember, we'll have a clear view of the ocean. We can talk about some things."

They went out of the lounge and were met by a crystal-clear day, a light blue sky and calm, dark blue ocean beyond the beach. A large canopy covered the patio providing shade from the basting sunlight above as they sat and began to talk.

"You know, Erin," Sandra began, "the setting is so nice here with the beach and all. It's just like it was when I was here last time, coming to you with all the problems I had at that point in my life."

Erin said, "Yeah, I'm happy to see you here too. But I must admit I didn't expect you to be back so soon."

"I know exactly what you mean, Erin. But since leaving this place, I feel that God has given me a new lease on life, and I often dream about standing here on the beach with the man of my dreams, looking out over the ocean at a magnificent sunset.

"But despite my dreams, Erin, once I returned to Detroit, I thought I might never get back here to Bermuda. I guess I told myself that I could accomplish so much at home, dealing effectively with my health issues. So I was thinking, Erin, that there was no need to come back here—at least not so soon. But I was given an opportunity to return, and it was an offer I just couldn't refuse. Erin, I owe so much to you for all that; this place means so much to me. And all of us owe thanks to my friend Maggie's acquaintances, Courtney and Gates, because they're the ones who organized this trip in the first place."

Erin said, "Yeah, I'll have to thank them myself when I see them, especially Gates, since he's the one that made all this happen."

Erin redirected the focus of their discussion on Sandra. "You know, Sandra, I'm so glad you've put your life together since you were here last."

Sandra interjected, "But as you've mentioned to me on several occasions, Erin, it wasn't so much my efforts as it was through divine intervention that I regained my health. God certainly showed His favor when He allowed me to see those signs. That helped my confidence so much! But I realize now, with what you taught me, that it wasn't the signs that did it. It was my ability to believe, an ability that God gave me, I might add. And it was that belief that led me to live in agreement with Him as you and I prayed that day. At that point I truly believed that I was healed even though I continued to have the symptoms of being sick for weeks after that."

Erin was intrigued with Sandra's thoughts about maybe not returning to Bermuda. She gave a spiritual reply, saying, "Well, Sandra, you have learned a lot because you realized it wasn't me that helped you the most; it was yourself being willing to allow God to perform the miracles He did in your life. In other words, first you had to believe that God could deliver you—and that's exactly what He did—because of your belief. And frankly I don't understand everything that was involved. But because you believed, God was the one that healed your body. It's very exciting to know that God is willing to help us; we just have to believe and act on that belief. And that's exactly what you did when you responded to those signs we talked about."

Sandra replied, "Yeah, Erin, I told Mensie all about it long before she passed, and she in turn told it to Maggie. But beyond that, things have progressed rather well for me, and much of it has to do with me not having to worry about my illness. Well, let me make a correction, it's not *my* illness anymore. I've rejected all aspects of me being sick and have claimed my healing. And you know what? It was all made possible by being here with you. You know what I mean, Erin? I mean, with those signs you encouraged me to look for—the sands on the beach and the stars in the sky. You know, I've tried to tell this story at times to friends of mine back in Detroit, but I really don't think they believed all that I was telling them. But I know it was a miracle, Erin," Sandra said as emotions started to build in her spirit.

Erin listened patiently as Sandra continued, "Yeah, I know it was a miracle and that's all that counts. You know, Erin, I believed that at the time and even now I'm convinced that what happened was an act of God helping me to overcome the issues that I had of my illness as well as my emotional state then. Hallelujah!"

After that testimony by Sandra, Erin said, "You go ahead and cry, girl. With all that you've been through, it's important that you give God the praise because He delivered you." Erin handed Sandra some tissue so that she could wipe away the tears.

Once Sandra regained her composure, she said, "Erin, I don't mean to burden you. And …"

Erin responded before Sandra could say anything else. "Aw, you don't have to apologize for anything, Sandra. Let me ask you this," Erin said in an effort to change the subject. "What has your life been like over the past year?"

"Well, Erin, you know how thankful I've been for my deliverance. But you still have to live from day to day and deal with the various emotions that often come. One challenge I have now is trying to find someone I can share my life with on a constant basis."

"Yeah, Sandra, I think I know what you're talking about," Erin said. "You want a man in your life. Am I right about that?"

Sandra replied, "Well, Erin, I still get lonely sometimes. And I'm not ashamed to say that those feelings I used to have about being with a man… Well, those feelings still come from time to time. I think I've gotten over the feelings that I used to have for Maggie's husband Fred. I just don't look at him the same way. And I told him that—that I see him more now like a brother. I'm not sure how he took that, but that's how I feel now. So I've been able to control my feelings a lot—about him anyway. But sometimes, not often, mind you, those feelings do crop up on occasion, not about Fred now but just about having a man to confide in sometimes, not to mention the physical affection someone like that could provide. And I really yearn for that kind of affection when I'm depressed about something. You know, the times I get lonely and want the physical touch of man? I know that it's wrong, but sometimes I feel powerless to do anything about it. You know what I mean?"

Erin said, "Yes, Sandra, I do. Just keep praying."

With those comments from Sandra, Erin saw this as an opportunity to respond in a way that related to her own issues regarding this subject. She said, "I sure do understand what you're saying, Sandra. Actually, I'm in a similar situation. I mean, I don't have a desire to be with someone else's husband—nothing like that. But I too get lonely sometimes and would love to have a male companion. But again, Sandra, I think the key to a solution for this issue is to continue to believe that God has our best interest in His mind and that things will work themselves out for our benefit—either in the short run or the long run."

Erin continued, "Of course, as humans we tend to want things when we want them, which is right now. We don't want to wait.

But you know what, Sandra? One of the most important virtues of a believer is patience, having the ability to wait for the things you want, trusting that God will work things out for us to assure that our desires will be met the way He would have them be met. And let me tell you something else, Sandra: we are told in the scriptures to pray for our desires and believe that we've already received them—as crazy as that might sound. Yeah, that's a powerful kind of belief, the belief that you already have what you want, even though it may not have manifested itself yet in the physical. But guess what? You already did that in the case of your illness when you were here last. Now all you need to do is ask for what you want or desire beyond what God did for you before—fulfillment in your love life—a desire to have that man you want. Just believe that God somehow will work that part of your life out for your good as it says in the scriptures. Romans 8:28, I believe."

"Oh, Erin, that's so encouraging," Sandra replied.

"Yeah, the desire that you want now is not like what you needed last summer; that involved the healing of your physical body. And, Sandra, you let me know that need was certainly met, but now you have another desire—for a male companion. But the key again, Sandra, is to believe. Sincerely believe that your desires will be met and they will. That's what the scripture says."

Sandra took a few moments to adsorb what Erin had told her. "Well, Erin, I've been praying. But I think I see what you mean. It's not just praying and asking God for want you want; it's believing that He will give it to you if you trust Him."

Erin agreed with Sandra's assessment. "You're right, Sandra, and I'll tell you something else. If you really want to be radical in your belief, you have to believe that you've already received it even though it may not have manifested itself yet in the physical."

"Praise the Lord, Erin. You sure have made my day!" Sandra confessed.

"Yeah, Sandra, I believe that you will get the man you want *somehow*. And you know what: he might be right here at this resort, and you might even find him here before you leave in a few days!"

Sandra replied, "I hope you're right, Erin, and I will be looking."

"You got it, girl. That's the spirit!" Erin said encouragingly.

After those discussions about personal issues, Erin talked to Sandra about her stay at the resort. "Sandra, I need to tell you about your accommodations while you all are here at the resort. I'll let you get going in a little bit, because I know you'll probably want to take a snooze before this evening's dinner. But I have some good news for you. You'll be in a room of your own just like the one you had the last time you were here. In fact, it's the same room."

Sandra was excited about that news. "You've got to be kidding, Erin," she said. "I've got my old room back from last summer? I have so many memories in that room. And I'll tell you I did a lot of praying there, which I don't think I ever told you. But thank God those prayers were answered."

"Well, that's great, Sandra," Erin responded. "But let me tell you something else. To get you that room, you had to be placed in the quarters next to Wynn's friend's folks. I hope that won't be a problem."

"On no," Sandra replied. "I'll just stay to myself. But I'm sure they're nice people. I'll just have to play my radio a little softer. You know, girl, when I was last here, I just turned that thing up as loud as it could go, knowing that no one else was around. Remember? It was just you and me here at this huge resort because of the storm that was predicted to come."

"Oh, how I remember," Erin replied. "Yeah, you might want to keep it low this time. Well, everything is set with your lodging. Just get a key from the front desk, and the bellman has already placed your things in the room," Erin said.

"Okay, Erin. Listen, thanks again for everything," Sandra replied.

Erin in turn expressed her gratitude to Sandra and her group for being at the resort. "No, I want to thank all of you for being here this week. Well, let me get going, Sandra. I have a lot of work to do this afternoon in preparing for you and the other members of your group. And, oh yeah, that includes Wynn's friend Jeanie and her folks too."

With that they both went their separate ways with plans to reassemble for dinner later in the evening.

§ § §

Jeanie and her folks had just arrived at their hotel in downtown Bermuda when she received a call from Wynn.

"Hello, Jeanie. Did your family make it to your hotel safely?" he asked. After she responded in the positive, he continued, "We've been here for about an hour, and I believe most of us have finished unpacking."

"Well, we had a long wait for a hotel shuttle at the ship's docking area, but it finally arrived and brought us here to the hotel," Jeanie replied. "It was so hard loading the luggage we had onto the vehicle and then having to take it off once we got to the hotel. And David got so upset over it. Mom doesn't like his temper tantrums. I think he has anger issues, Wynn, but I haven't had the nerve to ask him about it. But we finally made it to the hotel," Jeanie concluded.

"Well, that's good you all made it to your destination," Wynn said.

Wynn got straight to the point after that. He said, "Jeanie, I want to tell you something about your lodging arrangements while you all are here in Bermuda. As I hoped, my mother's friend said the resort where we're staying would have more than enough room for you and your folks to join us here. And like I said back on the ship, things will be a lot more comfortable here than where you are. No doubt about that. So when you see your folks, could you tell them that we would be glad to have all of you join us? And you can tell them that one of the people in our group is a hotel owner and can take away any expenses that your folks might have because of the late change."

Jeanie felt excited by Wynn's proposition. "Okay, Wynn," she said. "Let me go tell my folks. I'll call you right back and let you know what they say."

Wynn responded, "Okay, Jeanie, you do that, but also remind them that there's a dinner at seven and we are looking forward to seeing them—and you too."

§ § §

Jeanie assumed that David and her mother would be unpacking when she entered their bedroom but discovered them embracing and being intimate with one another.

"Oh, sorry," she said, looking down toward the floor. "I came in at a bad time. I can come back later."

David blurted out, "No! No! It's too late for an apology. You've ruined it for the both of us. Well, what do you have to say?"

Rather reluctantly, Jeanie responded, "Well… Well, this friend of mine who I met coming here on the cruise said they're staying at a resort on the beach and that we're welcome to stay with 'em while we're here in Bermuda. And the best thing about it is that there's no extra charge to stay there. My friend is very nice, and the members of his group are nice people too."

David snapped, "Well, how do you know that they are nice? Have you met them?"

Sheri interjected, "Don't you believe her, David? I'm sure they're fine if Jeanie says so."

"Well, okay, so how about it, Jeanie?" he asked impatiently.

"No, I haven't met them, but I believe what Wynn told me about them."

David replied sharply, "And who is this guy Wynn?"

"He's the son of one of the members of their group."

"Well, you have a lot of trust in what this guy has to say. But I have to admit it does sound like it'd be a good arrangement. But let me ask you something else. Are they willing to pay our cost of reneging on the reservation that we've made to stay here? You do know that there will be a charge, don't you?" David asked.

Jeanie responded, "Yes, Wynn said that they would take care any extra expenses we might have because of the change. And that's because a friend of Wynn's mother knows someone who is a hotel owner and could easily take care of those extra expenses."

With that bit of assurance, David confirmed that he was willing to change their accommodations.

"In that case, yeah, let's leave this dump," he said. "I was just talking to someone earlier right off the street and showed him how common this place looks. But the way it looked in the newspaper before we left home, I thought that it was a great deal, and that's why I reserved it. But, yeah, let's go to stay with 'em, especially if there's no charge."

"Oh, that's great, David," Sheri said.

Jeanie was so excited and appreciative about David finally giving his approval for the change that she almost went over to give him a hug. But she thought about his past actions towards her, so she decided not to.

Figure 9: Front of Run-down Hotel

"Do not withhold good from those to whom it is due, when it is in the power of your hand to do so. Do not say to your neighbor, "Go, and come back, and tomorrow I will give it," When you have it with you." (Proverbs 3:27, 28)

Jeanie's mother responded, "David, I'm really glad you agreed to make a change. Yeah, this place was all we could afford. And I think we should be thankful to have gotten this place. At least we're in Bermuda. But wow! We're going to a resort!" she said with excitement. "And the reality is that, yes, this was all we could afford, but let's face it, there are other better accommodations than this place. And now we have a chance to be in one of them. I say let's go for it. Yeah, I'm with you on this one," Sheri said.

With everyone in agreement, David said, "I'll tell you what, Jeanie. You go back and tell your friend that we agree to their proposition. I can even initiate the change in our reservation and get that information to this hotel owner you're talking about. And if all the details can be taken care of this afternoon, we'll be there for that dinner that's supposed to happen at seven."

Jeanie said, "Okay, let me get going and I'll contact Wynn and let him know that you two are in full agreement. And, oh yeah, you can expect to hear from the owner soon after I call Wynn so that your expenses here can be taken care of before tonight."

"Okay, that's what I'm talking about, little girl," David replied. "Now come on over here and give me a hug."

Jeanie again was hesitant about hugging him. She said, "No, David, let me go to give Wynn the news."

As Jeanie was leaving, David said, looking towards his girlfriend, "Sheri, you'd think that girl is afraid of me sometimes the way she responds to my good intentions. Anyway, Sheri, let's start the repacking so we can get out of here."

"Okay, David," Sheri replied. "But as far as Jeanie is concerned, you just leave her alone."

Sheri didn't know if those words to David would limit his aggressive behavior sometimes toward Jeanie; she just felt she had to accept it.

Jeanie contacted Wynn after leaving her folks, and preparation began for their relocation from that downtown hotel to Erin's beach resort. After the news got to Gates that Jeanie's folks had agreed to be with them at the resort, he was able to communicate with David and take care of their reneging on the reservation at the downtown hotel.

§ § §

Maggie's group wanted to get some rest and recover from the previous two days spent on the cruise from New York. But Jeanie's folks spent the afternoon communicating with Gates to finalize matters concerning their release of payment for the reservation of their downtown hotel room. Gates even made arrangements for them to take the shuttle Maggie's group used to come to the resort earlier.

Because they had unpacked very little of their belongings, Sheri, David and Jeanie had only a small number of items to repack. In very little time they were able to have their luggage in front of their hotel where they waited for the resort shuttle to arrive. When the shuttle arrived, David was amazed at its size.

"Wow! This is a nice vehicle," he commented.

The driver placed their luggage in the back as the three of them boarded.

As they finally took off for the resort, David said, "Now I know what we've been missing by making reservations at that downtown hotel."

Sheri said, "Okay, David. You know what I said about complaining about what we got. And we're not at the resort yet. I have to admit though, I'm glad we got away from 'that dump' as you put it, David," she added in a joking fashion.

Everyone was eager to join Wynn's group in a much more serene, luxurious setting. The shuttle arrived at the resort in the late afternoon about 5:00—only two hours from the time everyone was to congregate for dinner. Erin was there to greet them.

"Welcome to Golden Retreat," she said. "And I take it that you are Mr. Lowe and you—you're Mrs. Lowe, I presume."

Sheri responded. "Yes, this is David and my daughter Jeanie. It's okay calling us Mr. and Mrs. Lowe, but I'll tell you a secret: we're really not married—at least not yet. But we plan to tie the knot very soon by going to the Justice of the Peace," Sheri said as her head turned toward David and smiled.

David didn't respond but rather said a brief "Good afternoon" to Erin.

Sheri continued, "We just like the idea of being considered husband and wife. Don't you think that's so cool?" Sheri asked Erin partly in jest but somewhat serious as well.

"Well…." Erin said tentatively. "Anyway, it's so nice having you here." Erin paused and continued, "We're really grateful for all of you accepting our invitation to come here to the resort.

Sheri said, "No, thank you for inviting us. There's just no comparison between here and where we moved out of at that downtown hotel."

After Erin welcomed Sheri and her clan to the resort, she questioned their living arrangements in her mind.

"Well, it's great that all of you are here," she said. "We've met your daughter Jeanie and she's a fine young lady. And, yeah, that's no place to be on a vacation in Bermuda. Let me show you to your rooms, and Johnnie, our bellman, will assist me. Johnnie, could you come with me and bring their luggage to their rooms?"

"Sure, Ms. Erin," the bellman answered. Addressing Jeanie and her folks, he added, "You all just go with Ms. Erin, and I can take your things up on this special elevator we have."

David gave the bellman a tip and, along with Sheri and Jeanie, began to follow Erin to their room for their four-day stay at the resort.

§ § §

In about an hour, everyone would gather in the Shelling Room of the resort, the main dining hall. A large window provided a clear view of the beach and the ocean beyond. At that time of day, a spectacular sunset would blaze across the horizon.

As the dinner hour approached, members of Maggie's group began to funnel into the main dining area. Wynn and Katie were the first to arrive and got their seats on opposite sides at the end of an elongated table. They had rooms next to each other and walked to the dining hall together. Not long after that, Jeanie and her folks, David and Sheri, came in and without hesitation Jeanie went and sat next to Wynn.

David liked the idea of mingling with other members of the group, so he told Sheri, "Let's sit down here on the opposite side from where Jeanie is sitting and let her have some time alone away from us with her friend." She agreed and they went and took their seats.

With their seats secured, David decided to walk near a window for a smoke while other members of Maggie's group began to filter in. Maggie's friend Sandra took an end seat opposite Wynn. Soon David finished his smoke and went in the direction away from Jeanie to sit in the spot he had secured earlier, which happened to have been next to Sandra. Sheri was sitting on the other side of him. Within the next two minutes, everyone had gathered around the elongated dinner table. This arrangement of individuals made it convenient for the group to converse with one another. Erin was the last person to come in to take her seat; she stationed herself at the very end of the table near where Sandra was. They all would have ample time to chat as they waited on appetizers the waiter would bring.

As the appetizers came out, smoked chicken wings and biscuits, the discussions began.

"Well, Jeanie," Maggie began as she sat directly across from her. "It's so good that you and your family could come and join us here at the resort. I look forward to meeting your folks."

"Thank you Miss, Miss ..."

"Maggie," she interjected when she realized Jeanie did not remember her name. "But some people call me Mag. I'm delighted you all are here," Maggie said to Jeanie. "And by the way, just call me Maggie, not any of this Ms. Maggie stuff. It makes me feel old."

"Okay, Maggie," Jeanie reluctantly responded.

Katie, sitting beside Maggie, said, "Yes, Maggie, I've found Jeanie to be a nice girl."

Maggie responded, "Yeah, Katie, I can sense that, and it seems as though Jeanie and your son Wynn are getting along very well."

Maggie turned back to Jeanie and said, "Now Jeanie, what about your folks? I can see them sitting down there on the other end of the table."

"Yes, Miss Maggie. I mean Maggie," Jeanie said, still not completely comfortable using her first name. She continued, "Yeah, that's them all right." She looked in that direction.

Noticing that she was being talked about, Jeanie's mother Sheri yelled softly, "Hello, Maggie. I'm sure we'll get to talk some later."

Maggie responded, "Yeah, Ms. Lowe. We're down on this end talking with your daughter, and she seems to be enjoying herself."

Sheri said to Maggie in particular and to everyone else in general, "It's all right for you guys to call me Sheri."

David was carrying on a conversation with Sandra, who was seated next to him with Sheri on his other side. Sandra had told him some of her story already, and they had spoken to the point of being on a first name basis. Still, there was something about him that irritated her greatly, so at one point she just turned her head away, hoping that would lead him to end their conversation. After a while however, because of his persistence, she continued to talk to him.

"Yes, David, I've been through a lot with my health as well as having an injury as a result of a car accident."

"Like I said, I'm so sorry to hear about that, Sandra," David responded. "I had a car accident a while back myself, and I don't think I've ever gotten completely over that experience. So where are you staying here at the resort?"

She said, "I'm in room 111."

"Well, what do you know?" he replied. "We're in room 112, so we're right beside you. By the way, this is my friend Sheri."

David nudged Sheri to get her attention, and she turned around, looked at Sandra, and said, "Hello."

"Hi, Sheri," Sandra responded.

Without any further dialogue with Sandra, Sheri returned to her discussion with Maggie.

After that terse introduction to Sheri, Sandra said to David, "Well, I was told that my room is besides yours, but don't worry about me being next to you all. I have a radio and tend to play it loud, but I'll try to keep down the noise this week. I won't disturb you."

"No, no! Don't worry about it," David said emphatically. He leaned over and whispered to her, "My friend Sheri is a heavy sleeper. And an explosion could go off and it still wouldn't wake her up."

Figure 10: Shelling Dining Hall

**"...He who eats, eats to the Lord, for he gives God thanks; and he who does not eat, to the Lord he does not eat, and gives God thanks."
(Romans 14:6)**

Sheri, who sat directly across from Maggie and Fred, was too involved with her conversation with Maggie to notice David sharing an intimate aspect of her sleeping habits as he sat right there next to her.

Sandra responded to David's comment in a whisper. "I'm not sure if she'd appreciate what you just said, David."

David just smiled and shrugged. He said nothing more about it after that.

Although Sheri was keenly focused on what she was saying to Maggie, she couldn't help detecting a hint of intimacy in the conversation between David and Sandra—even if she couldn't decipher everything that was being said. Sheri wanted so much for him to refer to her as his wife, not just his friend. She looked forward so much to their marriage.

Sheri noticed David and Sandra whispering about something, so she finally turned her attention to him. She had to figure out a way to ask him about his conversation with Sandra without being heard by the others. To accomplish this, she asked David to come with her to get a better view of the ocean outside that large window behind them. The spot where he had gone earlier to smoke would allow them to be far enough away from those gathered at the table.

Jeanie's folks excused themselves from the dining table and proceeded to go a few yards away into a corner to enjoy the picturesque view.

Now confident no one else could hear them, Sheri asked, "Who is that lady sitting next to you?"

"Like she said, Sheri, her name is Sandra, and she's a friend of the lady you're talking to. I think her name is Maggie, right?"

Sheri replied, "Yeah, her name is Maggie."

David continued, "Anyway, Sandra was telling me about a car accident she had, and I told her about my own accident several years ago. You remember me telling you about that, don't you?" he asked.

Without responding to his question, Sheri said, "Oh, so you two are already on a first-name basis?"

David started to answer when they noticed the waiter bringing the food to the table.

She saw him too and said, "Well, let's go back to the table. We can talk about this later."

When they returned to their seats, Sheri saw what she had ordered and said, "Oh, I'm so hungry. I could eat a horse."

David replied, "Be careful of what you say, Sheri. That may be what you are eating. It was steak that you ordered, wasn't it?" David asked with a grin.

"Don't be silly, David," she said, still irritated over his discussions with Sandra. She told him, "Yes, I ordered a steak, so I'm sure it's beef."

Their discussion ended rather abruptly with that.

§ § §

"Oh, that ocean," Katie said as she gazed past Wynn at the view through the massive windows. "It's just mesmerizing. But I see some clouds in the distance, and I think it's the beginning of a weather system that's headed this way."

Katie directed her attention to Maggie, who was seated beside her. "It's not supposed to arrive here until later tonight and early tomorrow morning," she said. "I saw a weather forecast earlier today."

"Yeah, I think you're right, Katie," Maggie replied. "In fact, I think it's supposed to be very stormy with some rather heavy downpours and lots of thunder and lightning too by early tomorrow morning."

After savoring their meal, the group knew the time had come for the waiter to bring dessert. By the end of the delectable final course, more than two hours had passed since they sat down to dine at 7:00. They had left the dining area and returned to the lobby to carry on conversation. By 10:00 everyone was back in their rooms and contemplating their activities for the next day and for the remainder of their time in Bermuda. It was a glorious first day and night for everyone, and each of them hoped it would continue after getting a well-deserved good night's sleep.

Figure 11 Clouds

"For Your mercy reaches unto the heavens. And Your truth unto the clouds." (Psalm 57:10)

REFERENCE

"The Lord is slow to anger and great in power and will not at all acquit the wicked. The Lord has His way in the whirlwind and in the storm, And the clouds are the dust of His feet."
(Nahum 1:3)

5. SUMMER BREEZE

The rain and thunder rolled on into the early morning hours as predicted in the local weather forecast, but it did not interfere with the rest that everyone got on their first night at the resort. The weather system was short lived, and by daybreak the sun had risen above the eastern horizon.

As Gates and Courtney awoke on the second day in Bermuda, she said, "Gates, I'm sure glad things turned out the way they did. At one time I didn't think that we'd be able to satisfy that requirement of having four couples as stipulated in the agreement. But with Sandra being able to partner with Erin at the resort, everything worked out fine for them. We even got a fifth couple in David and Sheri."

"Yeah, things definitely did work out. But you know, Courtney, I do have some concerns about Jeanie's stepfather, David, or whoever he is. I mean, I'm still not sure about his relationship to Jeanie and her mother. I sat in front of him last night at dinner and did not like the way he was coming on to that lady Sandra, her being single and all. He claimed to be a special friend to the lady sitting next to him, Sheri, but he barely spoke her the whole time while sittin' next to 'em. And the language he was using… It wasn't very good, cursing and all. Let me put it this way. He wouldn't be mistaken for a choirboy."

After listening to her husband's rant about David, Courtney interjected, "Look who's talking. Now, Gates, you know how you were before you came to know the Lord. You didn't use, let's say, *perfect* English yourself. In fact, you didn't even believe in God; you were an atheist!"

"Okay, Okay, I get it! And don't remind me of those days," Gates responded to his wife's comments.

Courtney didn't let him off the hook so easily. "Yeah, and don't be judgmental," she continued.

"I'm just observing what I see," Gates said. "It's not that he can't change. I'm a witness to what God can do with a life that's not going anywhere but down under, if you know what I mean. But what I saw, Courtney, was not good," Gates reiterated.

After that discussion they both put the issue to rest.

§ § §

Because of his status as a hotel owner, Gates was able to select one of the executive suites at the resort. He chose the suite for himself and Courtney that allowed for a direct view of the ocean from its patio, one of only three such suites. The other two were pre-reserved for some other executives that would be arriving later in the week.

After Gates and Courtney rose and had a cup of coffee, they went on the patio outside their room and were met by a constant breeze coming in off the ocean. It was a remnant of the brief storm that occurred earlier in the morning. The summer wind refreshed their senses and reflected the serenity that they both felt on this second day on the island. The sound of the undulating ocean was intoxicating as they sat on the patio chairs viewing the soft blue sky with the waves washing the shoreline before them. They couldn't wait to go out and walk in the sand and to let the lapping water tickle their toes. Joyfully anticipating that reality, they both went back inside to put on their beach attire.

Courtney and Gates went the short distance to the downstairs lobby where they had been with the others the night before. Soon they ventured out on the beach. They were so far away from Detroit where nothing like this exists. They were content with the sand warming their feet and a bit of the cool refreshing ocean dancing around their lower extremities as they allowed the water to come up only to their ankles. They just stood there, holding hands, and admiring the sunrise beyond the horizon. This was their heaven on earth.

Figure 12: View of Ocean from beach

"...Fear not, for I have redeemed you; I have called you by your name; You are Mine. When you pass through the waters, I will be with you; And through the rivers, they shall not overflow you. When you walk through the fire, you shall not be burned, Nor shall the flame scorch you."
(Isaiah 43:1,2)

They left the water to search for an area where there was little traffic of beachgoers. After situating their beach chairs in a comfortable position, they lay there enjoying the view of the white sands and the ocean beyond as the summer breeze made its way onto the shore. With an umbrella protecting them from the bellowing sun above, they stayed there for a long while, relaxing as they watched others who were experiencing the same exhilaration as they did while walking through the sand and ocean waves only minutes earlier. Gates fell asleep amid the warmth of the sun and the sound of gently crashing waves. Courtney caught up on a novel she had brought on the trip to read. She dove into Fred's first book about his time in Hawaii.

The two of them stayed on the beach until lunchtime. As Courtney lay there beside Gates, reading her novel, she occasionally glanced up to observe the ocean waves lapping at the sand. In the distance she noticed what appeared to be another cruise liner on its way to a destination. The calm summer breeze was so refreshing, even intoxicating. She tried to keep from falling asleep like her husband.

Courtney then caught a glimpse of someone walking alone, apparently talking to herself. Courtney recognized the person.

"It's Maggie out there walking," she said to herself. She tried to get her attention.

"Maggie, Maggie, look over here," Courtney called in her direction, but Maggie couldn't hear her over the roar of the waves. After a few more attempts to draw her attention, Maggie finally heard.

"Courtney, is that you?" she yelled in bewilderment.

"Yeah, Maggie, it's me and Gates is lying right here beside me. You seem to be so much in your own world, talking to yourself and all. So, go ahead; I won't keep you from your thoughts."

"Okay, Courtney. You two continue to relax, and I'm gonna walk a little further down the beach before I start back to the resort. I'm sure I'll be talking to you later," Maggie hollered in her loudest voice as she headed farther down the sandy shore.

Courtney went back to reading her book, and Gates was in his own world too—sound asleep.

§ § §

As Maggie passed by Courtney and Gates lying there on the beach, she certainly had a lot to think about. She brought to mind the people in her life who had passed on. More than once she had questioned the fidelity of her previous husband John and the challenges they had in their marriage. Nonetheless, she finally had come to grips with the fact that John was always sincere to himself, and, she believed, to her. He accepted being in the limelight as a high-profile minister and the adulation that came with that position. The public renown seemed to have driven him—even to the point of disregarding his marriage to her in varying degrees, Maggie thought. She desired his attention on almost a constant basis.

For a long time, Maggie wavered between keeping her emotional ties to Fred, who was just a friend at the time, and remaining emotionally true to John, her husband. She tried her best, but those emotions kept getting in the way of her fully understanding John's stature in the community and his position in the church. She grew a lot from those times, and now, being Fred's wife, Maggie thought that she was a bit more accepting of her current husband's position as a writer and his need to spend a great deal of time away from her—much as John had done when she was married to him. She concluded that the notion of the grass being greener on the other side was not necessarily true because in relationships there will always be challenges and problems that crop up from time to time as a result of people's differences.

"If it's not one thing, it's another," she often said. Certainly Maggie had begun to realize the differences in the two husbands in her life.

The important thing to remember, in Maggie's estimation, was that in order to be truly happy she needed to accept these dissimilarities and move on with her life.

With the brief interaction with Courtney behind her, Maggie's thoughts had turned toward her sister Sadie as she started her walk back to the resort. Sadie had been taken away violently while still in high school. On occasions, she still thought of her sister as she was then—so vibrant and even rather brash, so full of life. Maggie remembered the eulogy Rev. John Sr. gave so long ago. He had described Sadie as her spirit having been released the moment that her physical life had ended. At that moment, there was no suffering, just a transition into the presence of God.

As Maggie continued her trek back to the condo, she decided to take a few moments to sit on the sand. With the soothing waters brushing her lower extremities and the calm breezes whistling by her, she thought deeply about her sister and what it all meant. Her pastor, Rev. John Sr., had given her such comfort then and again when he performed the eulogy at her mother's funeral much more recently. She remembered him giving her even more insight one day at a private conference in his office. As Maggie sat on the beach, continuing to meditate, she recalled that time. She mentioned to her pastor that she still had not completely gotten over her sister's death years earlier and vividly remembered how Rev. John Sr. tried to console her about the death of her sister Sadie, who had been gone for a long while. He provided solace in the more recent loss of her mother.

Rev. John Sr. had said, "You know, Maggie, only the spirit part of us and our physical body is limited by time, and, when that physical body dies, it returns to the dust of the earth eventually. And I say eventually because it normally takes time for this process to take place." He went on, "But our spirit is limitless and eternal as it lives on after our physical body perishes. As spirit beings, time is not a factor because in a spiritual dimension our spirit can be anywhere at any time, and we all are allowed to determine its presence without the limitations and restrictions of a physical body. But that only takes place at our transition."

Pastor John Sr. went on to refocus his thoughts from the individual person to God Himself. He continued, "You know, Maggie, the way I explained our existence at our transition a moment ago is the way God is and has always been. As the scripture says, to God a thousand years is but one day. So, spiritually speaking, our memory of those who have passed on is not altered by time. And that's why your remembering you and your sister being together seems only like yesterday, because in a spiritual sense it was not only like yesterday; it was like you're experiencing her presence right now at the moment those thoughts come to your mind! And that's very comforting," he added.

Not that Maggie understood everything that her pastor said to her that day. Even so, as he said, the thought was comforting. Rev. John Sr. explained that Sadie's spirit would be reunited with her physical body at the resurrection, an appointed time in the future. He also reminded her of another truth. He said, "And, Maggie, Sadie's spirit will be reunited with your spirit at the time of your own transition—when both of you will not be restricted by a physical body. Now let me just say that won't be any time soon; we all expect you to be with us, physically, for a long time."

Maggie felt the grains of sand prickling her skin and the calm breeze from the ocean whispered against her cheeks, cooling the heat from the sun. She continued to embrace the memories of the pastor's encouraging words and kindness.

"Another thing, Maggie," Pastor John Sr. had said, "as a minister I know about these things, but the knowledge I have is available to everyone. It's all outlined in the scriptures. Anyway, it's our spirit that makes up the physical body that we currently have and can even now reconnect with the spirit of the departed, that is if we have known them is our lifetimes. Do you remember, Maggie, the spirit that your sister had when she was alive, when her physical body was still with us?"

Maggie remembered her response. "Of course, I remember! I mean, she was really crazy sometimes, and many of us in the family didn't always understand her behavior. But we understood that she was a part of us and we all loved her, and we knew that she loved us, and most importantly we believed that she loved the Lord."

Her pastor had responded, "Well, her spirit is certainly still with you. Even now your sister's spirit is very much alive, and she can connect with your spirit now as well. In other words, she too is still with you—in spirit."

Rev. John Sr. had gone on to say that although inside a living physical body, the spirit can be anywhere it wishes through our imagination. Maggie could relate to that because even now, while obviously her physical body couldn't be taken back to her college days, her mind allowed her spirit to drift back to that time as though it was only yesterday. In the spirit, it was only yesterday. Whenever those thoughts came to mind, that reality became the present to the spirit part of her.

It was such a glorious time when she first met Fred. Even now on this beach hundreds of miles and many years from where and when it happened, that time they shared in that soda shop across the street from campus lived on vividly in her mind. Sometimes she could place herself right there again—in spirit—like the most real, tangible dream. At such moments time and distance suddenly disappeared.

The spirit could take her anywhere without the limitations of a human physical body. She only had to believe and imagine herself there. Maggie realized anyone could connect to the past through the spirit. Ultimately, all things were possible even those hidden desires. Most people might find it a difficult concept to conceive and believe because the spirit is linked to a physical body that is restricted to an earthly existence and to the material world. Maggie remembered Rev. John Sr. saying in a Bible class once that we only see through a glass dimly now in our earthly, physical existence and cannot understand everything. But the day would come when we would see beyond that limitation as we transitioned into a dimension where we could be even more aware of our surroundings than in our physical state.

§ § §

After thinking these deep thoughts, Maggie realized she needed to be getting back to the condo. Instead of continuing her walk back to the resort on the beach, she decided to take the street route. Her thoughts turned to the more practical rather than the mystical, and she said to herself, "Walking on this sidewalk is a lot better than sifting through all of that sand."

Along this route, she did a lot of sightseeing, viewing the other hotels, shops, and restaurants not to mention the high volume of traffic on the street. She shifted her focus from spiritual things to what was in front of her, the hustle and bustle of Bermuda away from the resort.

She realized that walking the beach allowed her to focus on the spiritual and provided good physical exercise as well, especially for her legs, and it increased her heart rate, something that physical therapists say is good for you. But it took forever, it seemed, to get where she wanted to go, sifting through the sand.

For the remainder of her journey after the long contemplation of what her pastor had told her about life in the spirit, Maggie spent walking on the hard surface of the sidewalk. It cut her travel time back to the resort in half.

But that first leg of her walk on the beach had offered an important opportunity to for reflection as she reminisced about John, about her mom, and about Sadie."

§ § §

While Maggie wanted to be back at the resort in time to have lunch with the group, Wynn and Jeanie arranged to meet to have their meal separate from everyone else. After having slept in their individual quarters late into the morning, they had agreed the previous day to meet in the lobby and talk a little before heading out someplace for lunch away from the resort.

Wynn arrived in the lobby first, shortly before 11:00, and sat on one of the large couches that were situated in the area. While he waited, he thought about questions to ask Jeanie about the living arrangement of her folks and how they were doing at the resort.

When Jeanie walked into the lobby area wearing shorts and a light blouse, she looked ready for the beach after lunch.

"Well, well, hello, Jeanie. Good to see you this morning. Did you sleep well last night?" Wynn asked.

"Yes, Wynn; I slept well. And how about yourself?"

"Like a rock!" Wynn responded.

Wynn asked her, "How have your folks been enjoying the resort so far?"

Jeanie replied, "They're fine. You can tell that they are happy not being in that place downtown."

Wynn wanted to get more detailed information, so he rephrased the question.

"Okay, Jeanie. I assume you're enjoying where you are now, but have your folks been getting along with the people in our group?"

Jeanie replied, "Like I said, Wynn, they're fine. They've been talking to people, getting to know some of your family and friends." She continued, "I understand last night at dinner David talked with your mother's friend Sandra. I've talked to my mom about it. In fact, we've talked a lot about his discussions with her, with Sandra I mean. And I'm not so sure how my mom is taking it. She's not jealous or anything like that, but she just doesn't want Sandra to be hurt. And more than that, I think she's really concerned that Sandra is alone— by herself. For the short time we've been with you all, I think all of us can tell that Sandra is the one person in the group who's not in a relationship. Everyone else is either married or a parent like your mother and my mom. David, well, David and my mom have only recently been together. I just hope it works out. I tried to tell my mother that there were other good men out there for her—better than what she got in the person of David. Anyway, my mother told me about what this lady Sandra said to David while they were sitting there having dinner, about her having been to Bermuda before. I just hope David doesn't mislead her and hurt my mom in the process."

"Well, you're getting a lot of information about Ms. Sandra," Wynn replied.

Jeanie talked to him in detail about her family. "But like I said, Wynn, I'm not sure about David's commitment to my mother. Last night, for instance, I heard what seemed to be some kind of commotion going on in their room. I'm thinking that since your room is next to theirs on the other side from where I am you probably heard something too. Did you?"

Jeanie rethought her question, and, before Wynn could respond, she said, "But wait a minute. I guess you didn't hear anything since you slept like a rock as you put it."

"No, Jeanie, I didn't hear anything," he agreed.

"Anyway, Wynn, it's useless to talk to my mother about David. And, oh, Wynn, I miss my father so much," Jeanie said.

Wynn could see the emotion starting to fill her eyes with tears as she thought about her natural father, who recently had passed. She gathered herself and continued.

"Our minister tries to comfort my mother from time to time by saying that he's looking down on us all. While I believe he's sincere in trying to help us, I don't know how much good it's doing. I don't have a lot of theological knowledge about the afterlife. Although I feel doubtful sometimes, I've heard so often the expression that 'when you're dead, you're dead' and that 'you only live once.' And seeing him so still and lifeless in that casket gave me chills. Oh my, Wynn!"

She became overwhelmed and started crying again at that point. When the sobs subsided enough for her to speak, she said, "But I do believe what our pastor says."

As Jeanie was about to give Wynn more detail, he tried to comfort her as much as he could, saying, "Well, Jeanie, my mother keeps telling me that you shouldn't depend on your feelings because your feelings will change. I mean she says it's natural to have those feelings of grief when a loved one dies. I know because I felt the same way when my father died. But my mother has a strong faith, and it apparently helped her get through a lot. I mean not only going through that but also dealing with other problems."

"What other problems? Your family seems not to have any problems," Jeanie said.

With Jeanie's last comment, Wynn was compelled to give some details about his mother's faith.

"Jeanie, my mother keeps telling me that all you really need to do to solve a problem is to simply believe that the problem has already been solved."

Jeanie interrupted Wynn at that point. "Now wait a minute, Wynn. That doesn't make any sense! Now how can that be? How can you believe you have something when you really don't have it?" Jeanie replied in a tone almost of ridicule.

Somewhat dismayed by her response, he answered, "Well, Jeanie, don't knock the messenger. I'm just telling you what my mother says to me a lot. Anyway, most of what she talks to me about she says is in the Bible. And she talks about this particular verse of scripture quite a bit. I think it's in the eleventh chapter of Mark, and I think it's the twenty-fourth verse in that chapter. And like I was saying, she claims that you ought to believe that you have something before you actually have it."

Wynn got excited himself as he continued. "Wow, Jeanie, after saying it that way like my mother, I have to admit, it does sound unbelievable! But again, Jeanie, I do know this much and that is she also says that's why we're called 'believers.' And that's because we believe what the Bible says about things. And I know from going to Bible study that the Bible says some amazing things. Going back to that verse of scripture that I was telling you about, I now can easily remember where it is because it was my age at the time. It was Mark, chapter eleven, verse twenty-four. Look! It's right here in the Bible I have."

Figure 13: Open Bible in Young Man's Hands

"All scripture is given by inspiration of God and is profitable for doctrine, for reproof, for correction, for instruction in righteousness. (2 Timothy 3:16)

Jeanie said, "Oh, so you're twenty-four."

Wynn responded, "No, but I was eleven at the time when I heard her talk about it."

"Wow! You have a good memory. That's all I can say. And I've never been around a guy like you before. You seem so mature. And your knowledge of the Bible—that's really cool. Anyway, I didn't mean to interrupt; please finish your thought. And by the way, I didn't mean anything by questioning your mother's knowledge of the Bible. I just never heard of it being put that way."

"No problem," Wynn said. "Think nothing of it."

Wynn continued his original thought. "Yeah, if you think about it, it's pretty wild what my mother says about how you should believe you have something when you don't actually have it. But if you really think about it, it's not that difficult to understand when you consider that anyone who works on a job believes in their minds that they have the money due to them even if they haven't received the check yet. At least they believe it if they continue do the work. That is, they believe they will be compensated for what they're doing. Otherwise, they wouldn't be doing it—at least most people. But I don't know of anyone who will work for free! Anyway, people know that they will get the money that they're working for. They just have to wait to get the physical check on payday."

Wynn continued, "Jeanie, you can look the scripture up that I was talking about for yourself and make your own judgment."

Jeanie responded, "You know, Wynn, I understand what you're saying. Sometimes you have to believe that you'll get what's due to you while not having received it yet. And as far as my father is concerned, I certainly hope that he is okay up there in heaven where he is. But that's all I can do," she said as the tears again flowed freely.

"Sorry about my emotions, Wynn," she added.

"No, you're fine, Jeanie." He could feel her sadness and wanted to ease it somehow. "Take these tissues and dry your eyes a little," Wynn said.

Although he was almost embarrassed to talk to Jeanie about something so personal, he felt compelled to share with her how Maggie had helped him with an issue of his.

He said, "I'm really impressed with your faith, Jeanie. Just continue to believe that somehow things will work out. Believe that your father is okay now and also that one day you'll be able to see him again."

He paused for a few moments and then continued. "Miss Maggie helped me with other things too. She talked to me once about the loss of my father, trying to comfort me the best she could. And she told me about a problem that I had, a problem that I didn't even realize I had at the time. And that was my anger. Jeanie, I had a pretty bad temper, but Miss Maggie helped me a lot with that. She simply told me to concentrate on the positive things in my life instead of the negative. And you know what, Jeanie? I believe that it's been working because things that used to upset me don't anymore."

Wynn went on to explain more about how much Maggie had helped him. "You know, Jeanie, after Miss Maggie helped me with my anger issues, the lady went spiritual on me. That I didn't expect. She told me that you just have to believe in whatever you're hoping for, and if you do that somehow you'll get what you want. In my case what I wanted was to get rid of a bad temper. And like I said, I don't have that problem any longer. But I put what she told me into practice, and, because I took action, I gradually began to get rid of the problem. Yeah, that's what Miss Maggie tried to drive into me, to truly believe and not have any doubts about what I'm hoping for. She told me that when you're really sincere in your belief, God sees that. And when God sees your belief, He will begin to work with you to get free of any problem you might have. Now that's really powerful, Jeanie."

After that summation by Wynn, Jeanie said, "Well, that's really interesting. And I believe what you're saying. God knows everything, even what we're thinking deep down inside, so He really knows whether we're sincere about it or not."

Wynn replied, "You got it, Jeanie. And if you are sincere about it, God can really work miracles in your life. That's what Miss Maggie said to me. Anyway, Jeanie, that's exactly what you need with that fellow David, some kind of miracle," he told her. "Listen, let's start walking towards some place to get lunch at one of the restaurants away from the resort. I think there's one not too far from here."

"Okay, Wynn. You know you're very encouraging, don't you," she said.

"Well, I'm glad I can be of some help. Let's get going."

As they walked to the restaurant, Jeanie continued talking about David.

Wynn said, "Just keep an eye on him and make sure he's treating your mother right."

"Okay, Wynn," Jeanie responded.

They continued their journey to lunch at one of the local restaurants. They also looked forward to some fun time on the beach.

§ § §

When Maggie finally got back to the resort hotel lobby from her excursion on the beach, she was met by Courtney, Katie, and the newcomer to the group, Sheri. As she normally did, Sandra had decided to remain in her room and relax and forgo travelling with the group, hoping to later talk with Erin about old times when she was last in Bermuda.

Erin was busy in the resort kitchen working with two cooks preparing dinner for that night.

When Maggie finally entered the lobby, she saw her friends and said, "Hello, ladies. Are you ready for lunch? And Courtney, I just saw you on the beach!"

Courtney replied, "Yeah, Maggie. After talking with you when you were out there walking, I remembered that we had mentioned going to lunch—us ladies, I mean. So right after talking with you I woke Gates up, and we came back to the resort, hoping to do just that."

Katie spoke up, "Yes, it's noontime, and I also remember we discussed going to lunch. If I recall, we talked about going shopping too. So, yeah, we can go out to the local mall, and I'm sure there are a lot of restaurants we can chose from to eat."

Maggie turned her attention to Sheri, saying, "So, Sheri, are you good with doing some shopping this afternoon? It probably won't be until later when we return here, but we'll be back in time for dinner. Erin is helping with that now."

Sheri replied, "I just love hanging out with you girls. It's so much more fun being here at the resort than it would have been at that downtown hotel. I thank you all for accepting me, David and my daughter Jeanie."

Thinking that Jeanie was with her son Wynn, Katie said, "Speaking of your daughter Jeanie, she's probably with my son. When I talked with him this morning, he said that they would be skipping this group lunch thing that we planned and would be going out on their own. But the way it turned out, all of us ladies will be out too!"

Courtney realized one of them was missing from their group of ladies, which prompted her to say, "Sandra will be here all by herself."

"You know, ladies, Sandra loves being by herself and she'll be fine," Maggie replied.

Katie said, "Well, what about the men? What about Gates and Fred? And, Sheri, where is David? What will they do?"

Sheri responded, "Oh, I know as far as David is concerned, he'll be fine. He'll figure out something to do. When we're at home, half the time I don't even know where he is anyway."

Courtney interjected, "Yeah, the men will take care of themselves. I know Gates will be going downtown to attend a meeting of some kind with hotel executives."

Maggie said, "Well, you know what Fred will be doing. He'll be writing on his new book. He's writing so much that I seldom get a chance to talk to him. But he'll be fine. Is everyone ready to go?" Maggie asked her friends.

Everyone nodded their heads in agreement.

Since everyone appeared to be ready, Maggie went to the kitchen where Erin was to let her know they wanted to take the shuttle to the shopping mall.

When Erin got the news, she went to get the driver to let him know that the group wanted to be taken to the mall. Maggie walked through a side door with Erin where they both saw Max, the driver. He was finishing up his washing and servicing of the vehicle.

Erin said, "Max, the ladies visiting with us will be going to the mall and need for you to take them there. So if you could take the shuttle to the front of the building when you finish, they can hop in and you can drive them."

Max replied, "You bet, Ms. Erin. You go back inside and tell them that the shuttle will be out front in ten minutes. I just have to gas up and I'll be ready to go."

Soon the ladies were off to do their shopping and to have some lunch.

§ § §

Except for Sandra, all the ladies in the group would be shopping at the mall. Most of the men found other things to occupy their time. Fred remained in his room, which was far from most of the others in their party, for most of the afternoon.

Except for Erin, Sandra felt all alone at the resort, so she spent time in the kitchen helping to prepare dinner. After that, she thought it could be like old times at the resort if she could play her radio as loudly as she did during her last visit to Bermuda when she and Erin were the sole inhabitants thanks for the impending hurricane.

When Sandra made the decision not go with the other ladies and remain at the resort, she did not think about Sheri's partner David being so close to her right next door. He remained in their room alone, and the quiet gave him an opportunity to take a nap. At least that's what he tried to do.

In the middle of a deep afternoon sleep, he heard loud music coming from somewhere close by. It sounded as if a party were going on.

Sandra was in her room dancing all by herself to old R&B tunes. She had turned the radio up loudly, which was enough to wake David from his sleep.

"What in the world is going on?" he asked himself, not being fully awake yet. He had thought the ladies had gone shopping, but, when he was forced awake by the booming music, he figured they had changed their minds and decided to have a party in the lobby. Once he was fully awake, he resolved to go to see if that proved to be the case. He put a robe over his pajamas and started walking towards the lobby.

As David left his room, he finally arrived in the lobby and found, to his surprise, no one was there.

"Well, what do you know—no one's here, but I hear music coming from somewhere."

He began to walk back toward his room and in the direction of the music. It led him to Sandra's room. Not remembering it was her room, he started to bang on the door, hoping that the occupants could hear him over the loud music. He began hollering and said, "Don't you realize that someone's trying to sleep?"

Sandra was dancing so wholeheartedly while listening to the music that she could hardly hear David's voice. All she could detect was the banging on the door.

"My goodness! What's going on? Who could be banging on my door like that?" she asked herself, feeling highly irritated.

David decided to repeat himself even louder. "I said, don't you realize…"

Before he could finish his sentence, Sandra opened the door and suddenly found herself staring at him while wearing only her nightgown. Without immediately realizing whom she was confronting, she said, "Mister, why are you…" At that moment it dawned on her that she knew this man. She asked, "Wait a minute. Aren't you the fellow I was talking to last night? Yeah, David, it's you!" she said still in a state of shock over his identity.

David said, "Well, look who we have here." His anger turned into bewilderment.

Both frustrated in the moment, they quickly realized they were confronting someone they knew and felt rather embarrassed. David was the first to express himself in a non-confrontational manner.

He said, "Oh, Sandra! Yes, we spoke last night at dinner. I'd forgotten you were the one in the room next door."

By this time Sandra's anger had diminished and she began to smile at the whole situation.

"Well, are you going to apologize for banging on my door like that?" she said.

"What?! After you were playing your music that loud when someone's trying to sleep? But, yeah, I do apologize."

Sandra replied, "No, I guess you don't have to. I just didn't realize anybody was around, so I decided to play my radio loud like I did the last time I was here in Bermuda."

David said, "Yeah, I do remember you talking about that last night."

David finally made a comment on Sandra's appearance. "You know, I almost didn't recognize you in your nightgown and those rollers in your hair," he said with a grin.

David continued, "Aren't you going to invite me in now that I'm awake? I'd like to join your little party."

Sandra replied, "Now, David, you practically told me that I look a mess with my nightie on and rollers in my hair."

"No, no, I didn't mean that. I think you look kinda cute," David replied.

"Okay, enough of your compliments. What about your wife? Or is it your *friend*, Sheri? What would she feel about your being in the room of another woman?"

David replied, "You know, Sandra, at first when you were making all that noise, I thought that Sheri and those other ladies had decided not to go to the mall and had remained here at the resort to do some partying in the lobby. But when I got up to see where the music was coming from, I saw that they were not in the lobby. So I figured they had gone to the mall after all. But I still couldn't figure out where that loud music was coming from. That's when the music led me to your place."

Sandra said, "That still doesn't answer my question. And don't call my music *noise*. Listen, let me put some clothes on and take these rollers out. You're welcome to come in for a while."

David responded, "That's what I wanted to hear. I'll go back to my room and freshen up a bit and will return in about ten minutes. I'll stay a while and then go back to get in my own bed for a little bit before going out to the beach to enjoy the breeze. It also may be the only chance I have to take a swim."

"Okay," Sandra replied. "But this time don't bang on the door; just ring the doorbell."

After a few minutes, David returned to Sandra's room. After she let him in and they took their seats, she asked, "So, David, aren't you being deceitful to your wife—I mean your friend Sheri, knowing that she probably wouldn't be pleased with you being here with me?"

David responded, "Well, I wouldn't call it being deceitful. You know, Sandra, ever since I talked to you last night at dinner, I knew there was something special about you. And…"

Before David could continue, Sandra replied, "Yeah, I'm someone special, all right. I've been converted. I'm saved, saved by the blood of Jesus."

David responded, "Well, that's not what I've heard. I heard that you like to party, and you proved it, Sandra, by playing your radio so loud. And I'll bet you were dancing and carrying on in here by yourself. That's not acting Christian-like to me."

Sandra responded simply, "Yeah, but you don't know me."

David said, "Well, I think I do."

He began to reach towards her face and said, "I know that mole you have on the side of your face is kinda cute, and…"

Before he finished, she warned him, "Take back your hand because if you don't you might draw back a nub."

David quickly retracted his arm after that and said, "Ooh! You're pretty feisty too, talking cutting someone's hand. Okay, I'm cool," he said.

Sandra tried to make David more comfortable by saying, "I didn't mean to startle you. I guess that's my old New York personality coming out of me."

David replied, "Okay, I can live with that." Then he started to ridicule Sandra's newfound faith. "Listen, Sandra, I may not know you well, but I've seen others like you with all this religious stuff and everything. I think it's for the birds. You have to have a life—to have some fun, okay?"

"But I do have a life now. And it's fun too. I just get a little lonely sometimes," she said.

"Well, I can cure that problem!" David confidently proclaimed. He calmed himself a bit and added, "I'm sorry, Sandra. I shouldn't be talking to you this way."

Sandra replied, "Don't apologize, David. But I'll tell you this. It's so much better for me than before the accident and before my illness as I told you last night." Her brow pinched slightly, a look of unease on her face. "But I do have concerns about Sheri, about how she would feel with us being alone together like this."

"Well, you're not that concerned, now are you? I mean, we're still together now, aren't we?" David said as he moved closer to her.

§ § §

Later that afternoon Erin finally finished her preparations for dinner. It would be in the same location as the night before, but a different menu would be offered. Erin went outside on the patio and sat in the chair overlooking the ocean as she and Sandra had done many times on her friend's previous visit. But Erin grew more concerned over Sandra's isolation from the rest of the ladies in the group. She could not understand why Sandra didn't integrate herself more with the group.

But Erin had her own issues. She yearned to be back in the States, to do something different from her current work an executive of a beach resort. As they continued to communicate with one another after she returned to Detroit, Sandra had presented her with ideas of returning to the States and had strongly suggested that Erin take up roots in the Detroit area. But Sandra realized that she probably wanted to remain in a tropical environment, so Florida would definitely be more desirable than Detroit with its long harsh winters.

As Erin pondered these considerations, she saw Sandra walking in her direction from the lobby. Erin thought this might be an opportunity for her to discuss the possibilities more. At least she hoped to do more venting to Sandra and get some encouragement from her as she had given Sandra during her previous stay.

As Sandra got close to her, Erin said, "Sandra, I was just thinking about you. Come on over here and let's talk. You sure do look somber, and what are those tears doing in your eyes? Aren't you enjoying yourself?"

"Erin, I treasure being here with you again. You know you practically saved my life the last time I was here. I'm just filled with emotion," Sandra confessed.

"Yeah, Sandra. I know you had a change in life when you were last here, and I'm surprised that you'd still be so emotional about it."

Sandra responded, "Well, Erin, it's not just that experience; it's what I've experienced since being here in Bermuda the second time around. Don't get me wrong; this place is still beautiful. Just look at the ocean out there and the summer breeze that's coming in from it. It's really heavenly. Erin, I've learned that material things don't bring you happiness. It's staying true to God's word that does that. And when you're outside of that word, it affects your happiness."

"So what are you saying?" Erin asked. "Has something occurred that has affected your happiness since you've been here at the resort?"

Before Sandra could answer, she started crying again. During intervals when she gathered her emotions, she mentioned her time being with some of the members of the group—namely Sheri's friend David.

"You know, Erin, I feel so guilty, being with another women's special male friend."

Erin asked, "What are you saying? Are you saying that you've been intimate with the man?"

Sandra admitted, "Erin, let's just say that I've seen David. You understand? I feel so ashamed, Erin. He just came onto me so strongly. In a moment…in a moment of weakness, I felt helpless to do anything about it."

Erin replied, "I see. Well, it's nothing that can't be forgiven. After all, there's nothing wrong with having a close acquaintance, Sandra. Hey, listen, it's broad daylight! I mean, how much can you do in an afternoon?"

At that point they both saw the shuttle return from the mall with the other ladies on board.

Erin said to Sandra, "Hey, Sandra, take these tissues and clean yourself up. We'll talk about this a little more later. Let me go and greet the ladies, and you can come along in a little bit. I think you'll feel a lot better when you do."

§ § §

Erin approached the ladies as they were getting off the shuttle.

"Hello, ladies! How was your trip to the mall?" Erin asked.

Maggie responded, "It was great! I think everyone got something they wanted. And Sheri got a nice gift for her friend David. I think we feel a little guilty because the rest of us only got something for ourselves. But I think our husbands will understand. And I think you would say the same thing, Katie."

Katie responded, "Yeah I really enjoyed myself."

Maggie finally allowed herself to share what she'd been holding inside. "Fred is so busy these days," she said. "But I know my husband is a good man. He is a strong breadwinner and, just as important, he supports me. I remember when I first started my daycare, he was one hundred percent behind me."

Courtney spoke up and said, "Yeah, Gates is busy too with work in his hotel business. But I'm not complaining because, if it wasn't for him, none of us would be here this week enjoying the ocean breezes of Bermuda. In fact, he's in downtown Bermuda right now conducting business. I just hope he gets back in time for dinner tonight."

"What about you, Sheri?" Katie asked before starting to head to her room for some rest.

Sheri said, "When I left the room, David was about to take a nap. He even had his night clothes on. So I guess he's been resting all day.

But, you know, David is a night person, you might say, and I don't get to see him much. Anyway, he probably slept the whole afternoon."

After getting the answer to her question from Sheri, Katie jumped back into the discussion, talking about her son, "Yeah, you may not spend much time with your husbands, ladies, but I have the same issue with my son. I don't get to see Wynn much either. So don't feel that you're alone.

Sheri retorted, "But, Katie, that's your son, for heavens' sake! It's different when you don't see the person often that you're sleeping with. I mean, David is my special friend, soon to be my husband!"

Katie replied, "Well, I guess you have a point, Sheri. But at least you have a man. As for myself, I'm still looking. Anyway, I know that Wynn and Jeanie have been on the beach most of the day. At least that's what she said they were going to do." '

Erin said, "Well, I'm sure they're fine. They seem to like each other so much." Erin continued, "It's good to find that true love, girls."

"Well, Erin," Maggie said, "Don't discount yourself. You'll find the right fellow at some point."

Sheri said, "You just make sure he treats you right. I know that Jeanie doesn't think a whole lot of David. But he's a good guy. At least he won me over when we first met. He flirted with me to the point where I couldn't resist his advances."

Having wiped away the tears she had just minutes earlier, Sandra walked to where the rest of the ladies were. She listened to what everyone had to say, but she didn't say anything herself. Sandra was especially taking in everything that Sheri said. Sandra didn't have the nerve to tell them what had transpired earlier in the day while they were at the mall.

She thought to herself, *Good guy? That woman, his wife, his friend, whoever she is, should know better and I should have known better. I'll talk to her later.*

§ § §

Katie had said some time ago that she would be headed to her room, but she still carried on the conversation with members of the group. As she recalled the mention of nice sea breezes, she said, "Speaking of those ocean breezes, has anyone seen the weather forecast? I know that it's nice out here right now, but I was told by someone at the mall that those winds are a sure sign that we're in for what's call a nor'easter weather system coming in later tonight—towards midnight.

Erin commented, "That's right. A weather system is coming, but I didn't want to alarm everyone. Listen, we still have the rest of this afternoon and the early part of the evening. In fact, it's those ocean breezes that make this place seem almost like heaven. You'll see."

After a brief thought, Erin continued addressing the group. "You know what, everybody? I think we can move the dinner up an hour to have it at six instead of seven. What do all of you think?"

Everyone nodded to indicate it was okay. Erin continued, "We can let those not here now know about the change so everyone still can meet promptly for dinner at the new time. Anyway, like I said earlier, you all need to get some rest because we're in for an exciting night later. I think I'll get a little shuteye myself."

Erin made one more admonition to the group. "Listen, everybody. I know there's some interesting conversation going on, but we all have to get ready for dinner tonight. We don't want to stay up too late because you know that the system will be coming through later. Hopefully the weather will remain fine during the early evening, and we'll get a chance to go out on the patio—maybe even the beach before the storm hits. And having dinner early will help a lot."

She told the group present one more thing. "It's supposed to be a bright moon early on tonight, and the reflection of the moonlight on the ocean as the water glistens off its surface is really a sight to behold. Okay, I've already talked enough. Listen, I'll give everyone a buzz about an hour before six, the new time we're supposed to be at the dinner table," Erin added.

"Sounds good," Maggie assured her, and the others showed their approval by nodding their heads.

Katie said, "Yeah, I can let Wynn know and he can remind Jeanie to tell her folks."

After that, everyone was finally off to their rooms to get a little rest and freshen up for the evening.

§ § §

When Erin had finished her conversation with the ladies of the group, she returned to the kitchen to assist the cooks and put the final touches on dinner. Maggie returned to her living quarters and found Fred looking at TV in another area of their large room.

"Fred, have you finished your writing for today?"

"Yeah, Mag. By the way, how was your trip to the mall?" Fred asked.

Maggie told him about the trip and promptly put on something more comfortable so that she could take a brief rest before dinner.

"Go ahead and continue watching TV, Fred. I won't disturb you. I'm going to lie down a while, to just relax a little before dinner," she told him.

Fred asked, "So what time is dinner?"

Maggie replied, "Oh, unlike last night, it won't be at seven. Erin moved it up to six. But it will be in the same area where we were."

After getting the rest she needed, Maggie walked over to Fred on the other side of the room. "I had a good rest, Fred, but I'll tell you I'm really hungry with all the shopping we did. And sorry I didn't get you anything at the mall. I felt kind of guilty when Sheri said she had gotten her husband a gift."

"Oh yeah?" Fred responded sounding surprised. "She must care a lot about him, because he hardly paid her any attention last night at dinner. I noticed that his whole focus was on Sandra. Oh well, it's not for me to get into anybody else's business."

"That's right, Fred; you've got enough to take care of right here at home!" Maggie said in a critical fashion, longing for her husband to pay more attention to her.

"Okay, Mag, I get it. You're reminding me of how David acted last night towards Sheri, not paying much attention to her. Listen, I know that I haven't been paying that much attention to you lately mainly because of my writing. Am I right about that?"

After donning something more comfortable, Maggie moved closer to Fred. She desired to be intimate with him and answered the question he posed.

"You're right. I'll let you figure out what to do about it—what to do about not paying much attention to me," she whispered to him.

§ § §

Katie wondered what Wynn and Jeanie had been up to. After the ladies dispersed and went to their rooms, she stopped by Wynn's room and found that he had not returned. She decided to give him a call.

Wynn picked up his cell phone and said, "Hello."

"Hello, Wynn," his mother said. "How are you and Jeanie doing?"

"We're just fine, Mom. We're lying here on beach chairs taking advantage of the gentle breeze coming in off the ocean." He continued, "It's really nice out here, Mom. You ought to come out and take advantage of it. You know we only have one day left here in Bermuda."

Katie replied, "Yeah, you're right, Wynn. I may come out tonight after dinner. You know the weather is supposed to turn for the worst later tonight."

"That might be true," Wynn said, "but you couldn't tell the way the weather is now. This summer breeze you'd never get at home."

"Yeah, in New York there are no beaches like this," Katie responded. "Anyway you two be ready for dinner at six."

"At six?" Wynn asked.

"Yes. Erin moved our meeting time up when you two were away because of the coming bad weather."

"Okay, Mom. We'll be there at six. Bye."

§ § §

Sheri was one of the last ladies to make it back to her room. She was unaware of the fact that David had spent most of the afternoon next door in Sandra's room. When she got to her room, Sheri realized that David wasn't there. The bed hadn't even been made after his nap. Being tired herself, she got under the covers and took a nap until the time came to dress for dinner. As she lay there, Sheri wondered where David was. Not only was the bed unmade but Sheri detected a fragrance in the sheets that was foreign to her, and she could not figure out the source of the aroma.

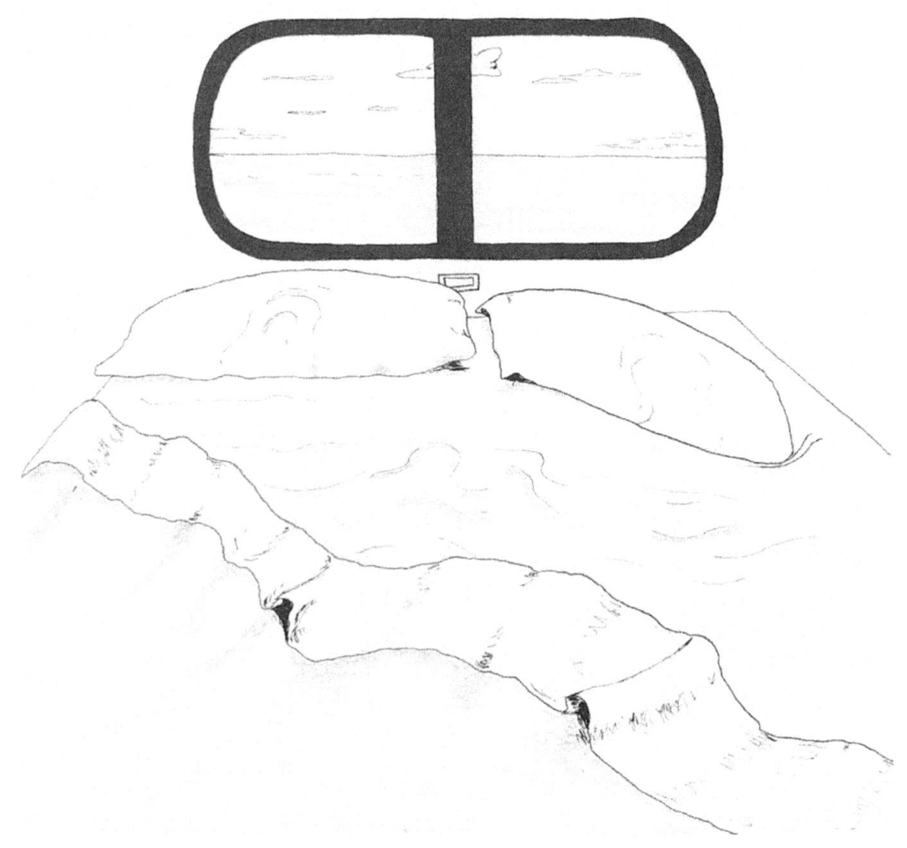

Figure 14: Picture of an unmade bed in room

"...you have sinned against the Lord; and be sure your sin will find you out." (Numbers 32:23)

While Sheri took her rest, Sandra found herself alone with Erin as the rest of the ladies had returned to their rooms. Erin was interested in what Sandra had to say earlier about her being with David.

Realizing this might be the only time they would have a chance to go onto the beach and reminisce, they strolled from the patio to a place near where Sandra had picked up a handful of sand on her last visit and Erin had said it was one of the signs she needed to confirm her healing. That was a moment to cherish.

But soon after they reached the spot, they saw David. As he had mentioned to Sandra in her room earlier, he had gone out onto the beach to enjoy the breezes.

As Erin and Sandra walked by, Erin said, "Hello, David. How are you?"

Sandra stared in another direction, pretending to enjoy the view of the ocean waves rushing onto the beach.

"I'm fine, Erin," David replied. "Who is the beautiful lady that you're with?"

Erin said, "Don't kid around, David; you know who she is. Sandra, the person you talked with so much last night."

Erin was unaware that he had seen her since then.

David said, "Hello, Sandra. You sure look nice today."

Not knowing exactly how to respond, Sandra continued to stare at the ocean and simply said, "Fine."

Realizing that Sandra was not about to carry on a conversation with David at that time, Erin interjected, "Well, me and Sandra are just walking a little here on the beach, but we'll be back at the resort soon to get ready for dinner. Don't be late now."

She forgot to mention the earlier dinner time.

"I'll be there," David replied. "Me and Sheri will be sitting in the same spot as we were last night."

The two women began to walk again with Sandra sauntering a bit behind Erin. All the while sneaking glimpses of David through half closed eyes. He gave her a brief wink as she walked away.

Erin and Sandra went a little farther to the place where they were a year ago when Sandra was last in Bermuda. The confluence of what had just happened to her only a short time ago when she was with David in her room and what happened at this very spot a year ago was too much emotionally for her.

Erin said, "Sandra, just think back as much as you can about the reasons you were here last time. You do know that in many ways your life was saved here last year.

Noticing Sandra's nervousness during their discussion with David moments earlier, Erin added, "Whatever may have happened today cannot cancel out that experience."

Erin's words comforted her. "Erin, I don't know what I would do if it were not for you," Sandra said. "You've been so helpful, which is the reason I wanted to come back to Bermuda in the first place. And Maggie gave me that opportunity with the help she got from her friend Gates, who arranged this whole trip."

Sandra continued, "So let me say this. What makes all this worthwhile is not the summer breezes that we're experiencing now or the beach or the thousands of stars that I saw that night that I later learned was a sign from God. It has been the feeling that I've had since then—the fact that I'm a forgiven vessel. And while it is difficult, I'll continue to have the faith that I need to get through this trial and all the other trials that I might have on this journey called life."

Not knowing exactly what trial she meant, Erin said, "That's the spirit, Sandra. Just remember, whatever you're going through, whether good or bad, there's always more, more good things coming your way! Now let's go back to the resort and get ready for dinner."

On their way back, they passed David again, but this time he had fallen asleep.

REFERENCE

"Not that I have already attained, or am already perfected, but I press on, that I may lay hold of that for which Christ Jesus has also laid hold of me. Brethren, I do not count myself to have apprehended; but one thing I do, forgetting those things which are behind and reaching forward to those things which are ahead, I press toward the goal for the prize of the upward call of God in Christ Jesus." (Philippians 3:12-14)

6. SUMMER STORMS

After everyone had returned to their rooms, little time elapsed before Erin's phone call to remind everyone of the new time they were to gather at the dinner table. Although Sheri was not in her room when Erin called, she was told about the new time by hotel staff about thirty minutes prior to 6:00. But David was still on the beach where Sandra and Erin had seen him earlier, defying the prospect that a storm was forecast for later that night.

After Wynn walked with Jeanie to her room, they went to see her mother in the room next to hers. She knocked and Sheri opened the door.

"Hello, Mom. Well, I'm ready to go to dinner. I said I would be here for the start of dinner, so here I am! I just have to change clothes and freshen up."

"Okay, Jeanie," said her mother. Sheri recognized her friend and added, "How are you, Wynn?"

Wynn replied, "I'm fine, Ms. Sheri." He added, "Well, let me go and freshen up a bit before going to dinner, and I'll see you two there."

Sheri said, "Okay, Wynn; we'll see you soon."

After Wynn left them, Sheri turned her attention to her daughter. "You know, Jeanie, I just woke up from my nap, but I'll be ready in a few minutes." She continued, "I don't know where David is. I suppose he's still on the beach. But we can go ahead to dinner, and he will be there later."

"Okay, Mom. Let me go inside, and I'll be back in a few minutes," Jeanie said as she needed to prepare to go to dinner. When Jeanie was ready, she returned to her folks' room, and she and her mother walked to the dinner hall. They arrived right at 6:00, the earlier time that Erin had suggested.

Everyone was situated in the seat that they had the previous night except for David. He wasn't there.

Erin said to Sheri, who had now claimed her seat, "Where is David? Didn't he get the message that we were to have dinner together at an earlier time tonight?"

Sheri replied, "Apparently he didn't. He said he was going to the beach, but where on the beach I have no idea."

Erin spoke up and said, "Sandra and I saw him this afternoon, sitting in a beach chair, but I forgot to mention the new time for dinner.

Sheri replied, "Well, he'll be here at least by 7:00 even if he didn't get the message. He probably thinks we're going to start at the time we did last night. I know he likes to talk, so he'll be here shortly."

Maybe he won't come at all, Sandra thought to herself. *I can't bear sitting beside him for another hour.*

Prior to David's arrival, the dining table was full of chatter as everyone talked about their stay in Bermuda. A joyful mood prevailed. Katie, who was located at the opposite end of the table from where Sheri sat, wanted to get some insight into how her son Wynn and Sheri's daughter Jeanie were getting along. So she left her seat and walked over to Sheri, taking what had been David's spot the previous evening. She found it easy to talk with Sheri, who was a quiet, unassuming person. Sheri told Katie she thought they were getting along well.

It was about fifteen minutes before 7:00 when Sandra noticed David entering the dining hall. Obviously her wish would not come true. David made a grand entrance almost an hour after dinner had started.

The festive mood of those at the dining table suddenly changed when David arrived during the middle of a discussion between Katie and Sheri.

Figure 15: David walking in dining hall with two women seated.

"A soft answer turns away wrath, but a harsh word stirs up anger." (Proverbs 15:1)

David approached Katie and Sheri. Putting his hand on Katie's shoulder for emphasis, he said, "Miss, you're in my seat, and I'd like to have it."

Sheri said, "Now, David, we're in the middle of a conversation."

It seemed that everyone at the table could hear what was being said. At the other end of the table, Wynn heard David talking loudly to his mother in a less than flattering manner. Wynn thought David was being downright rude.

Despite Jeanie's efforts to grab Wynn's arm and keep him in his seat, he got up and walked over to where David was. She couldn't prevent him from going to confront her mother's friend. Soon they were face to face.

At that point, Jeanie's fears were realized. Wynn was right in front of the man he felt was disrespecting his mother. Jeanie could only pray that things would not escalate.

Despite Jeanie's prayers, the confrontation was on when Wynn said to David, "Hey, Mister, don't talk to my mother like that! You know I think you're being very rude."

Realizing that things could quickly get out of hand, Katie looked up and said to her son, "No, Wynn; don't talk to him like that. I'll get up. I'll get up and return to my seat."

"No, Mom, this guy is just plain rude, and I don't appreciate it."

David turned from Sheri and Katie, who was still sitting in his seat, and looked squarely into Wynn's eyes. Turning his head slightly, he said, "For heaven's sake, who are you, dude?"

Sandra and all the others at the table were stunned.

Without much hesitation, David continued before Wynn could answer. "You'd better listen to your mama, boy!"

At that comment Wynn began to inch closer to David's face. That's when Jeanie's prayer that things would not escalate any further was answered because someone else got involved. In an effort to calm things, Gates, who was sitting across the table from Katie and Sheri, came and stood next to David.

He said to both David and Wynn, "Now, the both of you, cool down. We're trying to have some fun tonight."

Gates said more directly to David, "Listen, David, like I said, you need to cool down. I'm sure Katie will give your seat back. Didn't you hear her? She said she was going to get up and return to her seat, so you'll have your chair back. There's no need to cause a disturbance here."

David said, "Disturbance? Disturbance? Now I'm causing a disturbance? Okay, someone's in my damn chair and *I'm* causing a disturbance?"

Jeanie was thankful the confrontation now didn't involve Wynn. It seemed to her that Gates' focus was on David. She later learned that Gates was an experienced security officer who knew how to gain control of the situation.

David finally gave up his attempt to get his seat and instead decided to leave. He yelled, "Come on, Sheri and Jeanie. We're leaving. Let's get out of here!"

Sheri seemed helpless to do anything.

Erin shouted, "Oh no, David, don't you all leave." She tried to convince him to stay, but he seemed to have his mind already made up.

Extremely embarrassed by what was transpiring, Sheri got up and started to follow David and made a gesture for Jeanie to come with them. As the family left, Sheri shrugged her shoulders as she glanced at Erin. As they walked towards the door, Sheri asked in almost a whisper, "David, where are we going?"

He stopped and said in a louder voice, "I don't know but we're gettin' outta here!"

They headed to their room and finished the packing they had already started. They would later catch a taxi back to downtown where they would have an overnight stay at a hotel on their last night in Bermuda. At least one person was satisfied with this outcome, and that was Sandra. She got her wish that David wouldn't be sitting beside her at dinner after all.

Meanwhile, Wynn was torn between his perception of how David was treating his mother and the prospects of him not seeing Jeanie again. David had taken her from him.

§ § §

After the confrontation, dinner conversation became subdued. The group had liked the idea of Jeanie's folks forming that extra couple that Gates was so proud of. At least the minimum number of couples remained at the resort, satisfying the requirements that Gates needed to have the cruise in the first place. But everyone had enjoyed having Jeanie's folks, especially Sheri, who was adored by the ladies in the group. Her quiet demeanor seemed to be in contrast to most of the other ladies' personalities. And she differed considerably from David. The ladies felt that Sheri was victimized by an unstable man who showed signs that he really didn't care much for his relationship with her. Everyone seemed to have an opinion as to why things turned out the way they did with Jeanie and her folks.

David's need to be in control wasn't felt by anyone more than by Sandra, who allowed David to enter her personal and even intimate space. What was she thinking? The pursuit of happiness can take us to some uninviting places. For Sandra, that place was having a desire for someone to love her, someone who was similar in lifestyle and personality. In a moment of weakness, Sandra felt that David provided what she needed or at least what she thought she needed at the time, a man that she could identify with who had an interest in her. The only problem was that David was someone else's man.

You would think that Sandra would have learned her lesson after her desire to be with Maggie's husband Fred. Her pursuit of Fred led to a car accident when they both were in Minnesota and coincided with the diagnosis of an illness, both life-threatening scenarios for Sandra. Her previous trip to Bermuda when she met Erin changed and saved her life in Sandra's estimation. With the help of Erin, she gained the faith to overcome her illness. Now Sandra had to rely on that experience to rejuvenate her spirit and to exercise patience to get the desires of her heart.

After the commotion David created died down, she tried to lift her spirits as dinner continued but found guilt weighing on her. She uttered, "It's all my fault! Maggie asked me to come on this trip, and I've ruined it for everybody."

Maggie came to her defense. "How exactly did you cause David to act like he did? Don't feel that you're guilty, Sandra. He was responsible for his actions, not you," Maggie said reassuringly.

Erin jumped into the discussion. "Yes, Sandra. Maggie's right. You can't do anything about how someone else acts. After all, I'm as guilty as anyone, because if I had not forgotten to give David the correct time for dinner when we passed him on the beach earlier today, he would have been here at 6:00 when everyone else arrived. He would have been seated in his chair, and there would have been no confrontation."

Courtney, who had said very little on this trip, tried to correct both Erin and Sandra. "Don't either one of you accept the guilt that David should be carrying right now. I just feel sorry for his friend Sheri, who has to put up with this stuff on a daily basis. And she's thinking about marrying him?" she bemoaned. "I was right in front of them last night at the dinner table when he practically paid no attention to her," Courtney added.

Sandra retorted, "Well, you know why that was the case, don't you? I just led that man on last night while sitting next to him. I should have talked to Sheri more than what I did. But, no, I just kept talking to him as though she wasn't there."

Sandra began crying and uttered, "Sheri is so nice, a really nice person. I really love that woman as I'm sure all of you do."

Katie got into the discussion. She said, "Yes, we do love Sheri, Sandra, but don't you cry. We all feel the way you feel. What I mean is that I share as much of the blame as anyone. When we were at the mall, Sheri asked me my opinion of a gift that she was about to get for David. The item was a male bracelet with the inscription, 'You're so good.' I wanted to tell her how David was carrying on with you, Sandra, last night at dinner, and I wanted to ask if she thought he deserved the bracelet the way he was acting. But I didn't say anything. Besides, Sheri had to be aware of it, sitting right there beside him when he practically ignored her the whole time. In hindsight, I wish I had mentioned something about her buying that kind of expensive item for him. I should have discouraged her from getting it. But, no, I just said that I thought he would like it. Can you imagine that, knowing what we know now, any woman giving a man like David something like that? Yeah, I should have questioned her about getting it based on the way he treated her last night. You all saw it—how David practically ignored Sheri while loving up to you, Sandra. And, Sandra, I'm sorry to express my feelings about how he came on to you."

Sandra interjected, "No, no, Katie. You're right. He did play up to me a lot. But I didn't do much to discourage him. I should have been more sensitive to Sheri."

"Miss Sandra is right, Mom," Wynn said to his mother. "You can't blame yourself for something that weirdo may have done to Miss Sandra or even for what Miss Sheri did at the mall. I mean, when she made a decision to get the bracelet for that mother …."

Maggie interjected, "Now, Wynn, watch your temper. You've done so well up until now."

Wynn replied, "Okay, Miss Maggie."

"Well, what do the men have to say about all of this," Maggie said while turning her attention to Fred and Gates. They nodded without giving an opinion. But Gates said, "I think we've discussed this enough. We need to return to our rooms to get ready to leave tomorrow."

With that statement, everyone dispersed; they had completed their meal but most importantly they had a frank discussion about what had transpired earlier with David.

As everyone walked out of the dining area, Erin asked to talk with Sandra and Maggie. She said to them as they were leaving, "Hey, Sandra, Maggie, could I talk with you before you go back to your rooms?"

Maggie and Sandra agreed. Maggie said to Fred, "I'll be talking to Erin for a while, so be sure to pack everything so we'll be ready to leave first thing in the morning."

With that, Gates and Fred as well as Katie and her son Wynn went back to their rooms to start preparing for their departure the next day. Courtney had left earlier.

§ § §

Erin took Sandra and Maggie to the patio overlooking the ocean, her favorite spot on the resort. She had spent several hours there with Sandra the last time she was in Bermuda. Even when she was alone, Erin found the time to relax there, viewing the ocean and its waves beating onto the shore as gentle sea breezes wafted. Once she was situated on one of the three beach chairs, she along with Maggie and Sandra began to enjoy what was around them.

Once they were comfortably situated, Erin said, "Well, now we can talk and just relax while the weather is still pleasant. The recent forecast called for the system to arrive earlier than expected. But we still have time to view a brilliant sunset. Yeah, it's late in the day and soon the sun will be going down on that western horizon where the ocean meets the sky. And after that within, I'd say, about thirty to forty minutes, we'll be exposed to a starlit sky that you wouldn't believe. It's just beautiful." Then Erin thought, *how beautiful that sunset would be on a cruise liner, in the arms of the man of my dreams? Oh well.*

Figure 16: A Sunset

**"From the rising of the sun to its going down
The Lord's name is to be praised. (Psalm 113:3)**

Coming back to reality, and before the occurrence of that celestial event later, a starlit sky, Erin wanted to delve into the lives of Maggie and Sandra.

Before Erin spoke again, Maggie said, "Erin, you're at such an advantage being here to witness all this the year round. And, Sandra, I know you just took all of this in the last time you were here. That's what my mother always talked about. You know what I'm saying, Sandra? When you talked to her at length about your time here?"

Sandra said, "I'm just now recuperating from what transpired with David and how we lost those two beautiful women with him because of his antics. But I sure do remember that, Maggie, as though it was only yesterday."

Maggie continued, "Sandra, try as best you can to forget about what happened at dinner tonight. And, yeah, my mother told me a lot. She went into quite a bit of detail about what you told her of your experience. And, and …"

Before Maggie could finish, without explanation, she started to cry. Both Erin and Sandra said almost in unison, "Maggie, are you all right?"

Maggie responded, "Yes, I'm fine. I just get emotional sometimes when I think about my mother and how close we were."

Erin said, "Well, Maggie, one of the reasons I wanted to meet with you and Sandra was to talk about how you've been back in Detroit. I know that both of you have been through a lot over the past year or so. So I'll start with you, Maggie." Erin began, "I sure do share in the loss of your mother."

"Tell me about some of the things you're concerned about right now. I didn't tell Sandra this when she was here last summer. But I've been a spiritual advisor at the church I attend, and, quite frankly, it's my job to help people in their spiritual walk. Because, believe you me, the spiritual part of people is so important, and it affects everything else in a person's life, I mean, their day-to-day functioning in the world we live in."

As Maggie was getting ready to respond, Sandra said, "Erin, you sure didn't tell me that! I should have known with all the spiritual guidance that you gave me at the time."

Sandra's comments gave Maggie some time to ponder what Erin had asked her and consider what her response would be.

Maggie got a lot of encouragement from Erin. She felt that she could open up about some of the inner things that were most important to her. After some thought, Maggie said to both women, "Erin, I want to tell you something, and I want you to hear this too, Sandra. As I've confessed, I miss my mother very much. I've talked with my pastor about it, especially at the time just after she passed. He gave me all the words you would expect a pastor to give to a bereaving member of the church. I'm talking about things like 'she's in a better place' and 'she's in heaven walking on streets of gold, being with Jesus.' That's all fine and good, but it did little to ease the pain of the loss."

Erin responded, "I understand, Maggie. The pain is certainly there when it comes to the loss of a loved one. In fact, the Bible talks of 'the sting of death,' and I'm talking about the hurt that comes to all of us at a time when we lose a loved one. So I'm not denying the hurt that comes along with death, especially the passing of someone close to us. There's no way around it. Regardless of how young or old the person may have been or whether their demise was expected or not, it's a bitter pill to swallow. But it's okay to cry, to mourn. It's a natural response. But that doesn't do away with the hope as well as the peace that we as believers can have at such a time. Sometimes that's the only thing we can hang our hat on, you might say, and that is our belief, a belief that Jesus talked about in John 11:26."

Erin went on, "This peace I'm talking about can't be explained easily. And that's because the world often creates little opportunity to have peace. Just look at all the bad news on TV and in the paper. Let's face it: this world is secular, fleshly, with very little insight into the spiritual part of us, the part that can help us overcome even the sadness that results from the loss of someone we love. So as long as we believe, we can overcome the grief that we might have in these mournful times.

"So the solution to get all of us through times like these, Maggie and Sandra, is to recognize that the spirit is that internal part of us that never dies. It lives on and on even after we die physically, that is, after the body dies. The problem—at least the problem we have in the world today—is that the flesh part of us, the physical body, usually is our focus. Yeah, we're usually very concerned about how it appears, and the beauty industry is a testament to that. But, listen; there's nothing wrong with trying to look better, to take care of and enhance this physical body in any way we can. But we need to consider that there's another part of us, and that is the spiritual part."

Erin continued to give her insight to Maggie and Sandra. She said, "You know, Sandra and Maggie, those who have passed on, the spirit part of them is still alive and aware—probably even more aware than we are in this physical existence. But the way we are now, we have to share our spiritual essence with this physical body, and that is what the focus is for most people. We, as believers, however, are called to gradually increase our sense of the spirit while diminishing our physical aspects, which is very challenging to do in this secular society. So, Maggie, just continue to have faith, and try to place even greater value to your spiritual self, and you'll find a greater connection to your love ones who have passed on."

Maggie and Sandra were taking in all of what Erin was saying.

Maggie said, "Yeah, Erin, I think I know what you mean. Because today when I was walking alone on the beach, all I could think of was my mother, John, and sister Sadie, all who had passed on. Of course, I've had thoughts of other loved ones who have passed too, but the people I named were special to me, especially my parents. Anyway, what I thought about was their spirits, the spirit that they all had when they were alive in their physical bodies. And I'll tell you, Erin and Sandra, it was so comforting. And the strange thing is, I believe that they were communicating with me on a spiritual level.

But I'll tell you both something else, I think it took the serenity of my walking alone on the beach with no other distractions when I could totally focus on my spirit and the connection that I believe it made with their spirits. Somehow they became real to me as though they were there walking with me. I know all of this sounds kind of spooky, but to me what I experienced on the beach was so real. And let me tell you, Erin and Sandra, it was good."

Erin responded, "Yes, I believe you, Maggie. But you know what? That's all it takes to experience what you did when you were walking out there on the beach—to simply believe. In fact, if you remember in the scripture, that's what Jesus reminded Martha, the sister of Lazarus whom Jesus raised from the dead, that anyone who has lived and believes in Him would never die. He asked her if she believed it. It's interesting that she never answered the question that Jesus asked her. She only said back to him that she believed that He was the Son of God. But, Maggie, I believe what you've said about your experience on the beach today. I really do! I believe, Maggie, that in order to bring to reality what you experienced today out there on the beach, you simply have to believe, to truly and sincerely believe."

Erin went on, "Unfortunately, sometimes to believe is easier said than done, because there are so many distractions that we have to encounter from day to day. Plus, in our society, everything pretty much is catered to our physical existence. But, oh my, if we could get alone sometimes, like you did today, and just let that spirit part become more of a reality with us, it could bring unspeakable joy that the Bible talks about. It can do this even in the face of bereavement. As it says in Philippians 4:9, there is a peace that we all can have that goes beyond our understanding of how we attained it."

Soon Erin turned her attention to Sandra.

"Sandra, by now we know what your issue has been while here in Bermuda for the second time. That is, your issue with Sheri's husband David. But let's not talk about that right now. Let's talk about what has happened in your life during the past year back in Detroit."

Sandra said, "Well, Erin, as you know I went from here last year a different woman. And, oh yeah, I still had to confront the illness that I had. But I have to tell you, Erin, and you too, Maggie, unlike before I arrived here last year, I learned that God was personally involved in my life."

Sandra continued, "And, Erin, with your help, I received proof that God was involved with what I was going through because of those signs that I got when I was here. It was so emotional for me. So, when I left here, I had a new confidence in the face of the medical condition that I still had once I arrived back in Detroit. But praise the Lord! Here I am, Erin and Maggie, here in Bermuda again, not just existing but having a renewed purpose in my life, and that purpose is to do the best I can to serve Him, because He's done so much for me. It's too much for me to go into it all now, but all I can say is that I don't have the illness I had anymore. I've been healed of that! But all that started prior to my coming here for a second time, Erin, coming here and meeting David."

Erin responded, "Well, Sandra, I think you've learned that just because you've turned your life around spiritually, you still have that other part of yourself that's always with you, your flesh body. And, you know, the Bible teaches that there's a war going on between a believer's flesh and their spirit. That's why in the Bible even the Apostle Paul, who wrote more of the New Testament than anyone else, once said that this war was constantly going on in his life. He said that sometimes he did things that were wrong that he really didn't want to do. He was driven to do those things, as it says in Romans Chapter 7."

Erin continued, "Let me bring what the Apostle Paul experienced in today's terms. Do you remember, Sandra, this particular song, and I know you do because you listen to a lot of R & B. And the title of the song is 'If loving you is wrong, I don't want to do right.' Do you remember that song, Sandra?"

Sandra responded, "Yes, I remember it, but I must admit I didn't listen to it much."

Erin replied, "Okay. Anyway, you know sometimes the spirit within you wants to do what's right, but in certain situations our flesh won't allow it. But the good news, Sandra, is that, as believers, we can learn from our experiences, and do better the next time. And again, citing the Apostle Paul, we have to do what he says to make it work, and that is to put things that are behind us—to leave those things in the past and move forward with our future—as it says in Philippians 3. Jesus even said before Paul came along that whoever looks back and focuses on the past is not worthy to be a part of His kingdom. And I believe that scripture is at the end of Luke Chapter 9."

"Erin, you're giving so much wisdom just like you did when I was here before," Sandra said.

Maggie said, "I agree with Sandra. That's a lot of wisdom, Erin. But I want you to see something that's really nice. Look over there at the sunset. It's as magnificent as you said it would be, Erin. It's strange to see that orange reflection on the waters at this time of day."

Erin replied, "Yes, it's beautiful, and I was told that this happens just about every day. Very seldom are there clouds around to keep this from happening. And let me add something. Isn't it so romantic? I mean with the view and all. Just imagine yourself with your significant other viewing that sunset!"

Erin continued, "Oh, forgive me, Sandra. Let me get back to reality. Speaking of clouds, if you look in the other direction, you'll see some dark ones approaching us. Yeah, those are thunder clouds, all right. I was hoping to show you two that starlit sky, but I don't think that's going to happen. So, Maggie, it looks like you won't be seeing that beautiful canopy of stars that you always wanted to view. Maybe we should have gone out that first night. Sandra, at least you've seen it before. In fact, it was important in the healing that you received because of those signs that we talked about. Anyway, the wind has already picked up, so I think we should start to head back inside. By the time the storm starts to show its effects, we all will be in our rooms. Well, again, I might not rest right now because I have to help prepare the food for tomorrow morning."

Sandra offered a willing hand to help Erin in her preparations. "Listen, Erin, I'll come in and do a little something to help before I go to my room to retire for the night."

Erin said, "Okay, Sandra, but don't stay too long, because you need to get your rest, especially after the day you've had."

Maggie went back to her room and saw that Fred was up and writing again. As she walked in, she said, "Hey, Fred, are we all packed?"

Fred replied, "Well, some of it I packed but the rest I can do early in the morning."

Maggie showed her disappointment. "Oh, Fred, I was looking forward to a comfortable night of rest, not having to think about any packing. But okay. You finish what you have to do and I'm going in and go to bed."

Once Sandra returned to her room, she did a little packing and then returned to the kitchen to help Erin as she said she would do. She walked from her room past the lobby and down a narrow hallway to the kitchen.

"Well, here I am, Erin. Let me go over there and place this china where it should be. Just tell me what cabinet they should be in."

Sandra's body was there helping Erin, but her thoughts remained far away, replaying all the things that had transpired that day.

While helping Erin in the kitchen, Sandra said, "Erin, as I said earlier, I really appreciate all that you've done for us. And I'm really going to miss you." She started to tear up as she spoke. "I wish you would consider coming over to the States, and the Detroit area would be ideal. But I know that you're really accustomed to the tropical environment. So I'll be happy for you to be wherever you're content."

Erin replied, "Thanks, Sandra. We'll keep in touch, and I'm sure everything will work out for me just as I believe that things will work out for you. And, by the way, if I were to move to the States, I'd love living somewhere like South Florida where it's warm the year round. But that's just a fantasy of mine."

Erin continued, "Anyway, it's time for you to get your sleep. I can handle the rest of what I have to do. And remember what I told all of you the first day: if you have a problem in your room, just push the silver button near the center of the headboard on your bed, and that will alert me to come and research your issue. I'll know because I always wear a device in my ear to alert me to emergencies on the property. But don't be concerned should you have to use it, because it will activate a dim red light in the room."

Erin made a comment intended to make Sandra smile and uplift her spirits. "The red light might even put you in a good mood while you're listening to your music. It's just something that I've instituted around here to remind our patrons that an emergency situation of some kind is going on."

Erin assured Sandra, "It usually takes about five minutes for me to get from my room or any other area of the resort to any of our guest rooms after that red light is activated. When I get that signal, I usually arrive at the door where the signal is coming from, and I knock softly four times. And, you know, I then check my watch, and, if I don't get a response within about a minute after that last knock, I use my key to come in. I do that only if I don't get a response. Anyway, sleep well tonight," Erin added.

Sandra replied, "Okay, Erin. I'll see you in the morning."

§ § §

Because she wanted to remain and help Erin, Sandra was the last person in the group to return to their room. But really Sandra wanted to receive that last bit of wisdom that she knew Erin had and hoped that it would continue to make a difference in her life—much like the last time she was in Bermuda when Erin helped her to build her faith. In that instance, it led to a strength that she didn't know she had, a strength that led to her physical as well as her spiritual healing.

Sandra had done practically all her packing earlier, so she slipped on something more comfortable, donning a nightgown given to her as a Christmas present from Maggie. It certainly reduced the chill in the air that was produced by a cooling system that was centrally controlled.

Sandra could now lie in her bed and look back on all that had transpired since arriving in Bermuda for the second time. She turned on the radio, this time listening to soft jazz with the volume dramatically reduced from what it had been when David complained about the noise earlier in the day. That loud music had led to a compromise of Sandra's recently acquired values, principles that were instrumental in her healing. Now she could only reflect on those beliefs while still yearning to be close to someone who valued her as a person, someone worthy to be loved. Occasional distant thunder as well constant rain and howling wind interrupted her thoughts, bringing her back to the moment.

Sandra spent an hour in deep meditation hoping to savor as much as she could of the Bermuda experience—at least the pleasant activities of the past three days. She resisted sleep until shortly after nine o'clock when she heard a slight knock on the door. Being somewhere between waking and sleeping, she thought the knock was from Erin. After all, Erin told her that she would come and check on everyone at 10:00. But it was only just past 9:00.

Maybe Erin decided to come and check on everybody a little earlier than she had anticipated, Sandra thought. So she got up, went to the door, and opened it. The person she saw was definitely not Erin. It was David!

"David, what in the world are you doing here?" she asked.

David responded with his usual confidence. His thoughts were about finishing what he had started with her that afternoon and what he had planned to continue at dinner when he was interrupted by "that kid." He believed that now he had his chance.

With those conniving thoughts, David said, "Hello, Sandra. Now you didn't think I would have left you tonight at dinner without saying goodbye do you?"

Sandra replied, "David, keep your voice down. Someone might hear you."

"Now, Sandra," David began, "you must know by now my voice is always low when I'm with you like it was when I saw you this afternoon."

"Okay, David, let's forget about that," she replied. "How in the world did you get from where your family is—and I assume that they are someplace downtown—all the way here at Erin's resort with the kind of weather we're having?"

"Well, Sandra, sometimes a man will do anything for a woman he cares a lot for, and certainly a storm won't keep him away. And you fit that description," David said. "Besides, don't you think the weather we're having is making it that much more romantic?"

As he spoke, an immense clash of thunder boomed, and the rain and wind seemed to picked up significantly.

David said, "Speaking of my voice, you know by now that we're the only ones on this wing of the resort, since me and Sheri had our room next to yours and with Jeanie's room next to ours. But they're gone now. It's just me and you. You know, like it was before—like this afternoon when you disturbed me with that loud music you were playing?"

Sandra tried to change the tone of the discussion by focusing on Sheri. She said to him, "David, you mentioned Sheri. What do you think she'd say about this, about us being together like this? You know we've been through this before. I mean she is such a nice woman. You should feel fortunate to have her."

David replied, "But, Sandra, I'm fortunate now being here with you." He attempted to rub her cheeks with his fingers while he spoke.

Sandra said softly, "No, David."

Over the next few moments, the occasional thunder, persistent rain, and howling wind meant that a summer's storm was upon them. But it was a tempest in Sandra's life at that time as well, an inner turmoil between her flesh and her spirit. But in that moment of weakness, she remembered Erin's words about the silver button on the bed's headboard that she could use if she needed help. And, boy, did she need some help now!

As David made an advance towards Sandra, she said to him, "Wait a minute, David. It's kind of dark in here. Let me push this silver button on the bed's headboard and a dim red light will come on. You know, David, like you just said about the weather, it'll make it so much more romantic."

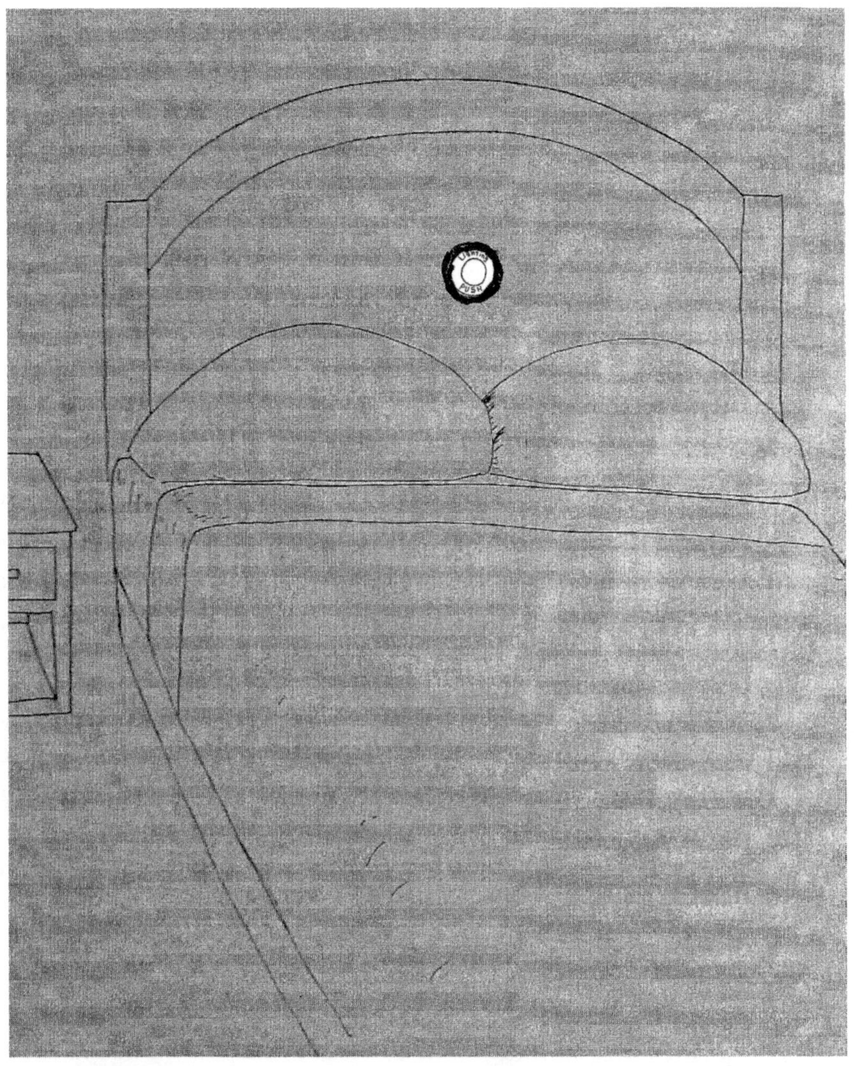

Figure 17: Button on the Bed's Headboard

"Make haste, O God, to deliver me! Make haste to help me, O Lord!" (Psalm 70:1)

David replied, "Oh, Sandra, you won't forget this night!"

As she pushed the silver button, he hovered over her. Sandra whispered, "I don't think you will either." She knew that soon they would be interrupted.

About five minutes passed after she pushed the button, and David had already begun to make his move on Sandra. To him, she seemed so willing, even suggesting a more romantic atmosphere with that red light. But it was only a deception designed to limit his advances. Nonetheless, he was more than willing to accommodate her.

As he pressed closer to her, they heard a soft knock on the door four times. At first David was so involved with his advances, he paid no attention to it. By the third and fourth knocks, he knew that they had been interrupted. That's when David said loudly, "What!" He asked himself in a softer voice, "Who could that possibly be?" In a voice that was little more than a whisper, David asked Sandra, "Are you going to see who that is at the door and turn them away?"

Knowing that it was Erin, Sandra said, "No. Just stay put for about a minute and they'll go away." Sandra remembered Erin had said that she would come to check on everyone at 10:00 unless she was alerted by a signal activated by a push of that silver button on the bed's headboard. Well, Sandra had done that about five minutes earlier.

Sandra knew that Erin would come in after about a minute if she got no response after the fourth knock. Suddenly it became quiet again, and David assumed that the person at the door was gone, so he continued with his advances, beginning to seal his intentions with a kiss. Sandra tried to delay what David wanted to do, knowing that Erin would enter shortly.

That's the longest minute, she thought after the last knock, eager for Erin to enter and rescue her from herself—and from David.

"David, David, don't rush things. You know it's even more romantic if you take your time and make this something you'll always remember," she told him.

David said, "Okay, I'll take my time." He added, "Yeah, with that red glow it sure makes things more romantic in here, Sandra, and like I said it will be a night that you'll never forget."

Just as David positioned himself on top of Sandra, Erin burst in and turned on the bright overhead. Her response to what she saw was predictable.

"Oh my, David. What are you doing here? And, my lord, what are you doing on top of her?" As she crossed the room, Erin added, "I'm calling the police; you're raping her!"

Now in panic mode himself, David replied, "No! No! It's not what you think!" He turned back to Sandra and asked her, "What is this? A set up? Sandra, what's she doing here?"

Without asking any more questions, David quickly got out of Sandra's bed, stood up to straighten out his clothes, and headed for the door of Sandra's room.

He said to Erin, "Stay calm, Erin; I'm gone."

As he began to walk out the door, David made a passing glance at Sandra and said, "I'll see you again."

With an outstretched arm pointing to the door, Erin said emphatically, "Out!"

Still shaken from the situation, Sandra refused to look at David as he was leaving. Now, having gotten up from the bed herself, she gazed down at the floor.

Erin asked, "Are you okay?"

Sandra just nodded as if to say that she was fine.

Erin said, "I don't think you'll have to worry about him anymore. I'll let the authorities monitor his every move on the cruise back to New York. Now you go to sleep."

With David's departure, that storm in Sandra's life passed, but the tempest outside persisted. It continued to roar—thunder, lightning and rain—until shortly before daybreak.

REFERENCE

"God is our refuge and strength, a very present help in trouble."
(Psalm 46:1)

7. *STORMY SEAS*

This last day in Bermuda started with a rising sun shining above the Eastern horizon. The storm that had persisted during the hours before daybreak had now vanished. Everyone got up early, ready for breakfast and the loading of luggage. Max had the shuttle in front of the resort to take everyone to the dock where their cruise ship would depart. Within an hour, the entire group started to board and say their goodbyes to Erin. '

"Enjoyed everything, Erin," Maggie said as she stepped into the shuttle first.

Sandra was the last to board and gave Erin a big hug. Emotionally drained from what had transpired the previous night, she said little but her embrace and expression conveyed more than words.

After they arrived at the dock, everyone followed protocol for boarding as they had in New York a few days earlier. As before, they agreed to meet when the boarding process was completed in the lobby area.

After making sure their luggage was securely in their cabins, the members of the group were ready for lunch. Gates was the leader of the pack and said, "Come on, everybody. That boarding process is very tiring. And it has made me hungry. Let's go now and get some of this good cruise food."

But before they walked a short distance to the dining area, Maggie wanted to announce an event on the cruise as it set sail to the ultimate destination of New York.

"Listen, everyone, there's a smooth jazz concert tonight, and everyone has been signed up to attend. I'm sure we all will enjoy it."

No one objected to the idea that Maggie presented. Now they looked forward to being together and having a good lunch to start their day.

As Maggie's group was about to enter the dining area, Gates said, "I see three empty tables over there by the windows and all of us can sit there."

"I'm with you, buddy," Fred agreed. "Come on, Maggie; let's get those seats over there near the wall."

The others followed suit and began walking towards that area where several seats were available. Once everyone had claimed their seats, off they went to the buffet to get every kind of food and drink imaginable.

§ § §

As had been the case when they cruised from New York on their way to Bermuda, one of the highlights was dining in the buffet area where a huge variety of foods and drinks were readily available. Eventually, everyone was seated and soon they were enjoying the meal and the view outside the window. There was a sense of sadness as the ship slowly began its sail away from the Bermuda coastline.

Figure 18: Three empty tables

"For every creature of God is good, and nothing is to be refused if it is received with thanksgiving; for it is sanctified by the word of God and prayer." (I Timothy 4:4,5)

Sandra took a final glimpse of the beach that dramatically changed her life the first time she was here. She tried to push from her mind the recollection of David sitting on a beach chair the previous day as she and Erin walked past. At that time, she could only sense his arrogance as he had asked Erin, "Who is that nice looking lady walking with you," knowing full well their intimacy only hours earlier.

Sandra felt so embarrassed about the entire experience, but anger also rose in her as she thought back on it. Sandra believed she had betrayed Erin's trust by her actions with David. Erin had become a dear friend and shared so much wisdom with her, insights that Sandra felt contributed to the healing of her body and soul. Erin's guidance revealed God's signs and His healing path to her. Seeing the immeasurable grains of sand on the beach and the multitude of stars in the sky had been signs of her healing. From them, she gained confidence that developed and strengthened her faith. Somehow she felt that assurance was shaken after what had occurred with David only hours earlier.

"Sandra, what are you thinking about?" asked Maggie, who was sitting near her at the dining table. "You seem to be in your own world, daydreaming and all. You really should start eating and enjoying your food."

Sandra replied, "I guess you're right, Maggie."

Sandra looked down and started to eat the food she had gotten from the buffet.

§ § §

Sandra wasn't the only one daydreaming at the lunch table. As Wynn ate, he couldn't help wondering if he would ever see his friend Jeanie again; he thought that he might never recover from David taking his family away from the group on that night at dinner.

Katie said, "Wynn, I know you have mixed feelings about leaving Bermuda. And I know you're thinking about Jeanie. Well, you may need to forget about her."

Wynn quickly responded to his mother's comments. "Mom, me and Jeanie got to know each other very well, and it hurts so much being away from her. And it's all because of that David. Do you know she's had issues with him ever since he met her mother, Ms. Sheri? Jeanie told me how he sometimes came on to her without her mother knowing about it. Can you imagine that? So it didn't surprise me that he came on to Ms. Sandra like he did the other night at dinner."

Wynn addressed the whole group by saying, "Hey, I didn't confront that man because of how he was acting with Ms. Sandra. I confronted him because he disrespected you, Mom."

Katie said, "Well, that's a noble thing you did, at least your intentions, but, Wynn, you need to avoid violence any way you can."

"I understand, Mom, but I'm still going to see her, one way or the other," Wynn assured his mother.

Sandra listened closely to what Wynn was saying. "You know, Katie," she began, "I never realized that David was such a womanizer."

Courtney jumped into the discussion. "Well, that's more than just womanizing, Sandra; that's molestation or child abuse when you're talking about fooling around with a young lady like that. I mean, how old is she anyway? Jeanie, I mean. She doesn't look to be a day over eighteen. And if she's that young, what that bastard did was on the border of molesting a minor. And you know what? You're talking about a criminal act! Yeah, that bastard needs to be in jail."

Gates added, "Well, let's not get carried away, Courtney. People are unfaithful every day, and it's kind of accepted in our society. But I'll give you this much: If it's a minor that we're dealing with here, yeah, he's in a heap of trouble! But I will tell you this, I knew that guy wasn't right by the way he was treating his lady friend, disrespecting her like that when he was carrying on there with Sandra."

Sandra said, "You know, Gates, I was such a fool for getting involved with him. I mean, engaging him so much at the dinner table with his friend sitting right there beside him. But for your sake, Wynn, I hope that you and Jeanie can somehow get back together."

At that point, Maggie got into the discussion. She spoke softly, saying, "Well, Wynn, I think you might get that chance before long because look over there and see who's walking into the dining hall."

It was David!

"Oh my," Katie shouted with a slightly louder voice.

As Wynn noticed that Jeanie and her parents were entering the dining room, his countenance changed dramatically. He immediately started to get up to go over to talk to his friend. But his mother grabbed his arm and pulled him towards her so that he remained in his seat.

She said, "Oh no, Wynn. This time you're staying here and not getting involved with that family now. You remember what happened last night when you confronted that man, don't you?"

"But, Mom, I'm not afraid of him like others seem to be. I'll kick his…"

"Now! Now! Let's be civil and don't get in the mud with a pig," Katie replied to her son. She added, "Wynn, use your head. Do you really think you'll be able to go over there and talk to Jeanie without her stepfather getting involved? I don't think so!"

Wynn replied, "Okay, Mom, but I'm going to see her somehow."

Sandra wanted to crawl under the table at the sight of David. Seeing him again so soon only served to increase her shame over the interlude with him.

§ § §

Sheri was the first in her family to notice that Maggie's group was seated across the dining hall; it was the first time they had seen each other since being at the resort. She said, "Oh, look, David. Over there is the group we were with at the resort—Maggie, Katie, and the rest of them."

"And, Mom, I see Wynn," Jeanie said. She continued, "Hey, David, couldn't we go over there and sit with them?"

"No, Jeanie," David responded. "I didn't tell you and your mother, but just before boarding I was asked to the administrative office of the ship, and I was told that I couldn't go near the lady who I was talking with at dinner on our first night in Bermuda. You know, that lady Sandra. So I guess we're off limits to them—what amounts to be a restraining order."

Sheri weighed in on the issue. "Oh, David, that's terrible that you are limited in your movements on the ship and have to stay away from wherever Sandra might be. By the way, why can't you go near her? What happened between you two?" Sheri asked.

Before he could answer her question, she added, "It couldn't be because of what you did at dinner that night. I mean, you only wanted the seat you were sitting in the night before. And Katie was willing to give it to you."

David replied, "Yeah, Sheri, but I guess they think I made too much of a scene that night. But I only wanted my seat." He left out the real reason he couldn't go near Sandra.

Sheri said, "Well, that's weird that you can't go near her since you had an argument with someone else. You know as well as I do that it was Katie you had an issue with, not Sandra, because it was her that was in your seat. And not only that but it was her son Wynn who confronted you. I just don't understand it," Sheri added. Her brow furrowed as she pondered the situation.

David didn't want her to have a clear understanding of what really happened with Sandra. He preferred to hide what he did with her in his attempt to become intimate with her after the encounter at dinner.

With the limited amount of information she had, Sheri reasoned, "That restraining order was an issue between you and Sandra for whatever reason. It says nothing about me and Jeanie communicating with them. So, David, I'm going over there and speak to them."

"Wait a minute, Mom. I'm going too because I want to talk with my friend Wynn," Jeanie said.

"Okay, Jeanie," Sheri responded.

David said, "You have no argument from me. You two go ahead and meet with 'em. I'm staying over here and getting my food."

Sheri and Jeanie made their way over to the group. As they approached, everyone was so happy to see the two of them. The ladies were especially happy to see Sheri because they got along so well with her when they all went to the mall back in Bermuda. They just couldn't explain why she would get such an expensive gift for that David given his conduct at dinner the first night when he flirted so shamelessly with Sandra in Sheri's presence.

Sheri addressed everyone there, "Hello! It's so good seeing all of you again. We really missed being with you all last night and this morning."

Maggie returned the compliment. "We're so happy to see you too, Sheri, as well as your daughter Jeanie. Why don't you two as well as your friend David come over here with us?"

Sheri looked directly at Sandra, and said, "No, I don't think that would be a good idea. David's not feeling well, and I think he just wants to be alone."

After Sheri's greeting, Katie said in a soft voice, "Well, we all can understand why David wouldn't want to come over after all that happened back at the resort at dinner last night."

She wanted to make a point by using her son. She said, "Now, Sheri, Wynn is over here…" As Katie looked around, she noticed that Wynn was no longer beside her and asked, "Where is that son of mine? I thought he was right here."

Fred said, "I think Wynn's having his own conversation with Jeanie right over there."

So much of the focus was on Sheri as she met the group that the two lovebirds found time to drift away from them and be by themselves to have their own conversation.

Katie continued, "Well, Sheri, I guess Wynn and your daughter Jeanie have a lot to catch up on."

Sheri replied, "Yeah, I'm sure they do have a lot to say to each other."

Sheri continued, "I wish I could stay longer, but we need to get back to where we're seated to have our lunch. Come on, Jeanie, we should leave now," she yelled to her daughter. Everyone in Maggie's group said their goodbyes in unison to Sheri and Jeanie.

They could see David in the distance at a dining table across the room, gazing at everyone there. Upon closer inspection, they could discern that his focus was on Sandra, who gave him only a brief glance periodically. Seeing him gave her an eerie feeling. A small part of her felt sorry for him.

Jeanie tore herself from the presence of Wynn and went with her mother back to where David was. But before they left each other, they had exchanged notes.

Wynn quickly scanned what she wrote and said, "Okay, Jeanie. I look forward to that." He smiled in anticipation of their next meeting.

§ § §

When Sheri and Jeanie returned to David, he asked, "Are you two satisfied now that you've seen your friends again?"

"Now, David, they're your friends too," Sheri replied.

"Okay, that's a nice little group. Too bad one of them took my seat last night at dinner, or we wouldn't be in this predicament."

Sheri replied, "You're talking about Katie? Well, you know it's her son that Jeanie really likes very much."

David said, "Yeah, I know. Well, he's not the only one in that group someone over here likes."

Sheri replied, "What? What are you talking about, David?"

David responded, "Oh, everyone in their group is nice, I'm sure," he said as he was trying to deflect his thoughts about having a special interest in Sandra, then stepped away for a smoke.

Soon they began their dinner, and a special announcement about the weather came on the overhead sound system. Later in the afternoon, they would make a stopover at an island in the middle of the Atlantic Ocean almost halfway between Bermuda and their ultimate destination of New York. The island's name was Little Fiji, which shared its name with the well-known island halfway across the world in the Pacific.

Then an announcement was made on the loud speaker of possible inclement weather in the area:

MAY I HAVE YOUR ATTENTION PLEASE. THIS IS THE CAPTAIN OF THE RHYTHM OF THE HIGH SEAS. THIS ANNOUNCEMENT IS TO INFORM YOU OF INCLEMENT WEATHER IS FORECASTED FOR THIS REGION OVER THE NEXT 48 HOURS. WE WILL KEEP YOU POSTED.

Upon hearing the announcement of the impending bad weather, David, who had returned to the dinner table from taking a smoke, said, "Oh man, I need to make sure I get a flashlight when we get back to New York."

Figure 19: David Went out for a Smoke

"Now he who received seed among the thorns is he who hears the word, and the cares of this world and the deceitfulness of riches choke the word and he becomes unfruitful. (Matthew 13:22)

Once Sheri heard his intentions, she said, "Well, David, I thought you were going to get that and some other supplies when you went out last night in all that bad weather that happened then."

David replied, "When I was at the local superstore, it was so crowded that I decided to go somewhere else to get those items. I went to this other store and they had run out of flashlights." David knew that he had to give some reason for being away from the downtown hotel for so long, having spent that time back at the resort with Sandra.

Jeanie paid little attention to their conversation. She had arranged a meeting with Wynn in a secluded area of the top deck in about an hour. So she wanted to finish her meal and return to the cabin to get ready.

She said, "Mom and David, I want to return to the cabin to freshen up; I want to tour the ship some before the storm arrives."

"Okay, Jeanie. David and I will finish our meal and figure out what we'll do next," Sheri said.

Across the dining hall, Maggie's group continued to enjoy their meal while viewing the coastline of Bermuda out of the dining room windows; the landscape of the island got smaller and smaller as the ship continued its sail further into the Atlantic. Little Fiji was still hours away, and cruisers again would have the opportunity to be on solid ground. They would be there in the day and during the early evening hours. The cruise liner would be off again just before midnight, sailing towards New York.

§ § §

With lunch behind them, most members of the group went to their cabins to unpack what they would need for their short layover in Little Fiji and their continued voyage. Jeanie and Wynn planned to spend their time together on the top deck until their arrival at Little Fuji.

After the members of the group left their lunch table, Wynn was anxious to see his friend again. He said, "Mom, I'm going to meet Jeanie on the other side of the ship."

As he started his walk from the dining area towards the top deck where they had agreed to meet, Katie asked, "Wynn, so you're not going to your cabin first?"

Wynn answered, "No, Mom. I'm going to a spot where we agreed to meet. I'll stay there until she arrives a little later. I'll just relax and enjoy the view until she gets there."

His mother replied, "Well, you don't have to tell me exactly where you'll be, but remember to be back in the cabin in time to prepare for the concert tonight. And, of course, we'll be getting off the ship tomorrow morning to tour the island of Little Fiji."

Wynn reassured her, "As I said, Mom, I'll be back in time for the concert. And I'm certainly looking forward to our time in Little Fiji later today."

After making his way to the top deck, Wynn was reminded of when he first started the sail to Bermuda from New York when he viewed the New York City skyline, which stayed in view for such a long time as the ship sailed further out into the Atlantic. This time, however, it didn't take long for the island of Bermuda to fade out of sight as the cruise ship sailed away from it. Soon there would be nothing but ocean. While continuing to scan his surroundings, the vast sea on every side, suddenly he felt a tap on his shoulder. When he turned around, he saw Jeanie.

She said, "Hello, Wynn. I'm so glad to see you again." She smiled and the sunlight sparkled in her eyes.

Figure 20: View of Bermuda Coastline from Ship's Window

**He shall bring forth your righteousness as the light, And your justice as the noonday.
(Psalm 37:6)**

Wynn replied, "Hello, Jeanie. It's nice to see you too. But, you know, I'm so embarrassed because of what happened at dinner last night."

Jeanie was sympathetic and replied, "Oh no! Don't be embarrassed about that. I know it seemed really bad and everything, but I learned from going to church back in New Brunswick that everything happens for a reason, especially if you know the Lord and try to do what He tells you."

"Jeanie, that's all well and good," Wynn began, "But how can something good come out of a situation where a stepfather is trying to hit on his own daughter, his stepdaughter, like he did with you? When he came to the dinner of supposed friends on only the second day of the cruise and disrupted everything like he did…. It's hard to get over that, Jeanie."

Jeanie replied, "Well, I understand why it's difficult for you to get over his actions. And I don't know why—why God would allow something like that to happen to one of His children. But you know, Wynn, that makes me think of something else that our minister talked about to his congregation. He said sometimes bad things happen to us that we don't understand. But our pastor said that's when we have to use our faith. In fact, Wynn, that's how we should live, according to Pastor Singer. That is, we should walk by faith and not by sight, knowing that, while in faith, everything that might happen in our life occurs for our good whether we realize it or not."

"Wow!" Wynn replied. "I've never heard stuff like that before, Jeanie, and I go to church every Sunday with my mother. I mean, they sing and shout, and the preacher preaches very hard and gets everyone involved in the service. And my mother really gets into it too, shouting and carrying on. She says we all need the Word to be inspired, but she also says it's an opportunity to give God the praise for what He has done for us. And I guess we do—praise the Lord, I mean. But it seems to me that you can praise Him without all that shouting and running around that goes on at my church. I even feel guilty sometimes that I don't shout along with 'em."

Jeanie responded, "Well, Wynn, there are so many churches out there, and each one conducts its service differently. But you know what? We all serve the same God, and really He's not as interested in the manner in which we worship Him as in the sincerity of our praise. Yeah, that's what gets His attention and allows Him to act on our behalf. That's why when we are sincere about our faith, doing what He tells us to do, He will do for us what we couldn't possibly do for ourselves in many cases. And you know? That's why we're called believers. Everything that happens to us will turn out for our benefit, and that's what we believe or at least should believe. Anyway, that verse of scripture comes from Romans 8:28, I do believe."

Jeanie continued to share some of her wisdom with Wynn. "And there's something else I want to say, Wynn, and that is church attendance is very good, our pastor says, because there's a benefit of being around other believers, those who think like you do, who share in the faith. But he also taught us that church attendance shouldn't be our focus as far as being a believer. He says that our focus should be in walking every day in His Spirit, the Spirit that's always within us as believers, the Spirit that leads us to do right and to avoid trouble. And, Wynn, we can do that whether we're in church or not."

Wynn responded, "Don't tell my mother that—that somehow church attendance is not as important as your belief. She's been in church all her life. With her, it's just something you need to do to be saved, she says."

After the last statement by Wynn, Jeanie attempted to change the subject. "Well, I know that your mother is a good person. But, you know, I realize that you're a good guy too, which is the reason I wanted to see you again. And I told David that, and he was good with it, believe it or not."

Wynn replied, "That's good to hear because the way he carried last night at dinner, I didn't think he would ever want to have anything to do with me again."

Jeanie repeated a sentiment that she had made earlier. "Well, as I said Wynn, he doesn't mind me being with you, and something else I want you to know is that my mother actually thinks a lot of you."

"She does?" Wynn asked. He felt encouraged by her words.

"Yeah, she does," Jeanie confirmed.

Both Wynn and Jeanie spent the next few minutes appreciating the cool breeze flowing around them. Jeanie reminded Wynn about the announcement she heard over the loudspeaker at lunch.

"It's so nice out here now, Wynn, especially with these gentle breezes, but I guess you heard about the storm that's coming later on."

"Yeah, it reminded me of the storm that we had last night that lasted well into this morning before daybreak," Wynn responded. "You know, Jeanie, all the thunder and lightning had the effect of putting me to sleep, so I slept through most of it."

Wynn and Jeanie spent another hour enjoying each other's company when another announcement was made about the coming storm:

THE CAPTAIN SPEAKING AGAIN. THIS IS A REPEAT OF THE PREVIOUS ANNOUNCEMENT OF INCLEMENT WEATHER. WE HERE AT CONTROLS ARE KEEPING TRACK OF DEVELOPMENTS AND WILL KEEP YOU INFORMED. THANK YOU.

With that, they decided to go back to their cabins earlier than they had anticipated. For Wynn, he knew he had to return in order to prepare to attend the concert in the main theatre of the ship.

REFERENCE

"For I know the plans I have for you," declares the Lord, "plans to prosper you and not to harm you, plans to give you hope and a future." (Jeremiah 29:11)

8. CELESTIAL WONDERS

Many cruisers spent the day on the top deck enjoying clear skies and the cool wind coming in off the ocean. There was no sign of bad weather, which almost never happened in this part of the world at this time of year. While the hurricane season started on the first of June at the time of the group's cruising to Bermuda, only clear skies surrounded them. But the first evening of the cruise away from Bermuda the weather shifted, not because of the impending storm due to arrive much later that night. A lunar eclipse that few knew anything about lay ahead of them.

§ § §

It was early afternoon when the calm breezes gave way to strong winds and a chance of rain. But the inclement weather was unlikely to arrive until later, so everyone was looking forward to the concert.

By 6:00 the group had assembled in the lobby of the main theatre and was ready for what they all had anticipated, an evening of smooth jazz. As they walked towards their seats, they began to sway back and forth as though they had consumed too many alcoholic drinks.

"Hey, Maggie, didn't the forecast called for bad weather arriving after midnight tonight?" Sandra asked. Before Maggie could answer, Sandra continued, "Why is this ship swaying back and forth so much? I can hardly keep myself upright! I'm grabbing at whatever I can find to keep me from falling. The bad weather that was forecast must have come earlier than they expected."

Maggie replied, "Yeah, Sandra, I know what you mean. It's hard for me to stay upright too."

Gates said, "And do you all hear that wind outside? Normally, you can't hear anything that's going on outside when you're inside the ship. So you wouldn't know what the weather is like. But that wind is howling out there! It almost pulled me out when I passed the double glass doors leading to the top deck as I was going to the restroom! It's weird because I know that the storm that was predicted isn't supposed to get here until after midnight, and it's only about 7:00. And just a few minutes ago when I was outside on that deck, the stars were out. Oh well, anyway, I'm ready for some good music."

Just before sitting down, Maggie said, "Fred, did you see that couple going out those double glass doors over there onto the top deck? I remember we went out there a short time ago, and we saw nothing but stars dotting the sky. It was such a beautiful early evening celestial light show with the stars being so bright that it actually brightened up the sky a bit. But, you know, the moon does that better than anything at least after the sun goes down. I just don't know where all this wind is coming from."

Then Fred said, "I know Mag. I stepped out into the hallway a minute ago, and I could hardly stay upright on my feet! I'm telling you, the ship is shaking to the point where it's hard to walk around without falling. And didn't we see the lady the fellow was with being interviewed with four other performers by one of the ship's hosts?"

"Yes we did, Maggie replied.

Figure 21: Slanted Hallway on the Ship

"My soul follows close behind You; Your right hand upholds me." (Psalm 63:8)

Then Fred continued to say, "But, you know, Mag, I don't understand the weather we're having either. It's not supposed to storm until after midnight. Oh well."

Since the show would begin soon, Fred and Maggie and the other members of the group staggered towards that section of the theatre where there were enough seats for all of them to sit together. The Mints had just left their cabin when they struggled to keep upright as they walked along the hallway. They hoped for an enjoyable evening of smooth jazz. They would deal with the weather when it arrived in a few hours. Everyone took their seats and waited on the opening act to come onstage.

Maggie, Fred, and all their friends enjoyed the show despite the rocking ship. Towards the end of the performance, the ship seemed as unstable as ever. Just after the last musical act, another announcement came over the loudspeaker about a coming storm:

> *MAY I HAVE YOUR ATTENTION AGAIN PLEASE. WE HAVE BEEN INFORMED THAT BECAUSE OF A COMING STORM, THERE WILL BE A DELAY IN THE SHIP'S DEPARTURE FROM LITTLE FIJI 'TIL TOMORROW NIGHT! AGAIN, WE'LL KEEP POSTED ON FURTHER DEVELOPMENTS.*

The announcement of an impending storm meant Maggie's group, as well as all the other cruisers, would have another day to stay in Little Fiji.

§ § §

After the concert ended, everyone returned to their rooms, knowing they would have an extra day of fun in the tropics. As Katie and her son Wynn went to their room, Wynn said, "Mom, it's good that we'll be here tomorrow because I know there are a lot of exciting things to do."

Wynn had a deeper reason for feeling delighted about the extended stay. He saw it as another opportunity to spend one more day with Jeanie before heading back to New York.

Katie replied, "Yeah, with this storm passing over later tonight, everything should be clear by tomorrow. At least that's what the weather forecast was saying."

The next morning, everyone went to breakfast. Fred and Maggie proved to be the early risers. When they arrived in the dining area near the top deck of the ship, no other members of the group were anywhere to be seen. They selected a table for four, the only one available at that time.

After getting their breakfast from the buffet, they were ready to partake when a young couple came to ask about the two chairs that were obviously not being at their table. Maggie saw that the fellow was staring at her, seeming to hope that she would offer him, and his female companion, the two available seats.

"Are these seats available?" the young fellow asked Maggie.

Maggie replied, "Sure; go ahead and sit down."

The couple accepted Maggie's offer and proceeded to get their food. When they returned to the table, Maggie introduced herself and Fred.

"Hello. I'm Maggie and this is my husband Fred."

The young man said, "Hello to you two. My name is Jake and this is a friend, Cindy."

Maggie said, "Hello, Jake and Cindy. I saw you yesterday when you were interviewed by one of the ship's staff members. I noticed you two going out on the top deck. You're a singer, aren't you?"

Cindy replied, "Yes, Maggie, I'm a singer. And I did my last performance last night."

Maggie said, "Yeah, it was probably at the time when we attended a jazz concert."

Cindy said, "You know it was so windy last night that it was difficult to stay upright while walking around on the ship. The ship was swaying so much I had to cling to the wall to keep myself from falling. I barely made it back to our cabin. Did it affect you two?"

Fred answered, "Yes, it affected us a lot, and, like you said, it was an adventure walking around on the ship. We knew a storm system was coming, but it wasn't supposed to arrive until much later. Well, I guess it arrived earlier than anyone expected."

After hearing Fred's comments, Cindy's companion spoke up. "Well, let me tell you. It was as clear as a whistle last night about the time you saw us go out onto the top deck. And, yes, it was very windy. But earlier in the week someone sent us a message that a lunar eclipse would be happening about the time you all are talking about last night. So we were expecting the eclipse, and that's why we went out when we did."

"Okay," Fred responded. "Now what does this lunar eclipse have to do with all that wind we had?"

Jake explained the phenomenon of the eclipse. "Well, I've been doing some research on it, and the best way I can explain it is that, when this celestial event occurs, the Earth is directly in between the sun and the moon. And when the three are in perfect alignment, a huge shadow is cast on the earth with the effect of the moon appearing as a huge orange ball in the sky. Because of the moon's strong gravitational pull on the Earth, it sometimes causes the air to move more than it would ordinarily, so the wind picked up a whole lot at that time."

Jake turned to Cindy and said, "I've always wanted to explain that to somebody ever since I learned it in a geography class back in college."

Maggie said to Jake, "Well, you seem to know a lot about the eclipse, and I guess you do since you took the subject in college. You obviously know what you're talking about."

"Yeah, so the weather wasn't a factor in all this, and there were stars shining brightly all around it. Keep in mind that if it were not for this rare alignment, people on Earth where we are would have experienced a typical full moon during this time of the month, a normal and expected celestial event."

Jake clearly enjoyed displaying his knowledge of the subject. "And that's what we saw when we went outside at the time you saw us last night. It was weird because it was kind of misty with the wind blowing very hard and everything. But when we looked up we saw the moon, not a typical, normal-sized full moon. Last night it was different. The moon was as big as we've ever seen it—like a huge saucer—like a spaceship that was orange in color hovering right above the ship! It was almost frightening! Yeah, it was like a spaceship hovering directly above us," he repeated for emphasis. "It was like something you would see at Halloween. We were alone out there, and I don't think anyone else got the word on it."

We've told of our experience to a couple of people, but I don't think they took us really seriously. After all, on a cruise like this, most people aren't that interested in an eclipse. I think you two have had more of an interest than anyone we've talked to," Jake said to Maggie and Fred.

§ § §

Beyond the rare lunar eclipse, the stormy conditions expected for later in the night caused cruise officials to delay departure by one day. Instead of leaving just after midnight the decision was made to reschedule for early the next night. By that time the forecast was for drastically improved weather conditions. So everyone was looking at an overnight stay on the island.

Maggie reacted to the news of a longer stay in Little Fiji with enthusiasm. "Fred, we're in for another day in the tropics," she said. "Isn't that great? I'm not anxious to get back to New York and then have that long drive back to Detroit."

Fred replied, "Yeah, it's nice especially when you think about how much writing I can get done."

Figure 22: Couple looking at large moon and the ocean.

As was the man of the dust, so also are those who are made of dust; and as is the heavenly Man, so also are those who are heavenly. And as we have borne the image of the man of dust, we shall also bear the image of the heavenly Man. (I Corinthians 15:48,49)

"Oh, Fred, you're always thinking about writing. Relax from all that and have some fun."

"Maggie, you know this is fun for me," Fred replied.

Maggie became irritated and said flatly, "Well, it's not fun for me. I want you to pay more attention to your wife."

Fred said, "Well, okay. We'll go and participate in whatever is happening now on this island while we're here." He continued, "I heard tonight's going to be nasty with a lot of wind and rain according to the weather forecast."

"Now that's more like it," Maggie said, pleased with his answer. "And maybe we can get someone else to hang out with us."

§ § §

Sandra had stayed in her cabin for most of the trip from Bermuda to Little Fiji. She spent her time listening to music and thinking about all that had transpired since she left Erin's resort for a second time. She thought about not only her physical healing, but also a total deliverance from her desire to be with Maggie's husband. The feeling this time was certainly not as good as it had been when she last left Bermuda. It was strange that she felt better then, even though at that time she had not yet been cured of her illness. But she was so filled with God's Spirit that the adversity of her physical illness didn't matter. Based on the signs she saw with Erin's help, she knew God would be with her going forward. Those signs confirmed in her spirit that she had been healed of her condition. This time, however, she didn't feel nearly as well after her second visit to Bermuda because she had strayed off the straight and narrow path that God had set for her.

Figure 23: Sandra's Thoughts

Such knowledge is too wonderful for me, It is high, I cannot attain it. (Psalm 139:6)

What a revelation! As the scripture says, it rains on the just as it does the unjust. The second time around certainly the rain fell on Sandra in the form of her near capitulation to David's advances. But with a forgiving spirit, she was truly sorry for her transgressions and understood that God had not forsaken her.

REFERENCE

"For He Himself has said, "I will never leave you nor forsake you." (Hebrews 13:5)

9. DISCUSSIONS

It would be about another hour before everyone would get off the ship and begin to explore Little Fiji. But Sandra knew that not much exploration was in store for anyone because of the coming storm. She said to herself, "At least storms in this part of the world are short-lived, lasting only for a few hours."

The weather forecasters predicted that this downpour would be gone by early morning. Sandra fully expected to take advantage of the pleasant weather after the storm. She anticipated enjoying some of the activities offered on Little Fiji, especially those that would lead tourists to venture into the local surroundings.

Until everyone arrived on the island, Sandra would be content with just sitting in her cabin and listening to the winds beginning to get stronger and stronger as she fantasized about her future.

§ § §

It was in the afternoon when the cruise ship finally arrived at the small dock of Little Fiji. Because of its small size, the one hotel on the island had been reserved weeks ahead for the cruisers. The hotel was a three-story stone structure with a large lobby. Behind it was a huge open area designed for concerts and various recreational activities for hotel guests, and beyond this to the west was the vast expanse of the Atlantic Ocean.

Everyone had their room assignment even before the cruise ship left New York for Bermuda six days earlier. As they did when Maggie's group first arrived in Bermuda, they agreed to come together, this time in a section of the lobby where they could be separate from other individuals and groups on the cruise. When they entered the building, Maggie led the group to a large fireplace to the right of the hotel's entrance.

Maggie's group of seven was a small portion of the hundreds of cruisers that were guests at the hotel.

"Wow! This is a wonderful place," Sandra said, "similar to Erin's resort back in Bermuda."

"Yeah, it's very beautiful here, but it doesn't have a mall that we can go to," Katie said.

Courtney responded, "Now, Katie, you know that we won't have the time to go to a mall anyway. Besides, this place is so small I'm sure it doesn't even have a mall. Plus the storm is coming."

Gates added, "I don't know about anyone else, but it's always good to be back on solid ground."

Fred said, "Yeah, Gates. I know what you mean!"

All Wynn could think about was when he would meet Jeanie again. Even before they left the cruise ship, members of the group had arranged to assemble after about an hour when everyone would be situated in their rooms. They had planned to gather in the lobby near that huge fireplace. Wynn remembered that Jeanie had told him

Figure 24: Lobby area of hotel

**But the Lord is my defense; and my God is
the rock of my refuge. (Psalm 94:22)**

her family had arranged to go on an excursion around twilight, so she would be committed to being with her folks later in the afternoon. They both knew they would have only a brief time together on the island at least on the first day in Little Fiji. So they tried to make the most of their interval together in the lobby. Once seeing her there, Wynn rationalized by saying, "I guess I'll just have to see her again tomorrow night once we get back on the cruise ship."

For now, Wynn was excited to share a few moments with Jeanie in the lobby of the hotel in Little Fiji around that fireplace. They knew with the coming storm everyone would hunker down in their rooms. Wynn and Jeanie talked for a while before getting settled in the hotel.

Maggie and Fred had arranged to go out later in the day to do some exploration of the island. Unlike Bermuda and on the cruise ship, the group did not plan to come together to eat as a collective. Everyone went independently about their leisure activities. There were several small restaurants and shops, even a convenience store, where people could eat, browse and explore. Most of the guests were content with shopping in the store to stock up on items they could have in their rooms to endure what was sure to be a stormy night.

§ § §

Eventually the midnight hour came, and everyone was safely ensconced in their rooms. The tempest was every bit as ferocious as the weather forecast had predicted. But everyone was tucked in, resting and riding out the storm as they waited for daybreak. For some in Maggie's party, the downpour was unsettling as they lay awake amidst the sound of constant rain, high winds, and occasional thunder. But for many, the howling wind and steady rain acted like a sedative, leading to a night of deep sleep.

Even at that late hour, both Maggie and Fred found themselves wide awake. Howling wind and persistent rain did not induce sleep. Instead, it brought to them a spirit of meditation, a reminiscing about their life up to that point.

Maggie was lying there on her back staring at the ceiling. She said, "We're lying here whispering to each other at midnight when we both should be asleep." She paused as the rain continued its music outside.

"Listen to that wind and rain out there, Fred. And how about the roar of the ocean. It's kind of soothing just lying here listening to the weather—the wind and the rain and all. It reminds me of the time when I went to my grandparents' house back in North Carolina when I was a kid. You know, one night it was so stormy it was almost scary, and my grandfather started telling us all those scary stories. But all that rain sure helped his garden to make things grow. Yeah, I can see it now – that old wood house they lived in, with the garden my grandfather had off to the side. But oh boy! When everything was harvested, we spent hours sitting in the front yard, just shelling butter beans, shucking corn, and heaven knows whatever other vegetables we worked with."

Fred didn't say much. He just lay there listening to Maggie. His parents taught him to stay as quiet as possible during a storm, that the Lord is doing His work. But Maggie continued to talk, reminiscing about her past.

"You know, Fred, my grandparents lived in this small town, and my grandfather had this large garden right outside their old wood house. Well, my mother used to visit them on some weekends, and I would go with her. I remember many times during late summer I had to shell butter beans in the front yard all afternoon. And, boy, did I get tired of doing that. Although most of the time the sun shined brightly, it sure was soothing under that huge oak tree. On occasion, very few occasions in fact, we would see someone drive up in the narrow driveway to pay my grandparents a visit. Those times were great because they gave us a reprieve from shelling all those butter beans. But after any visitors would leave, we'd go right back to those wooden chairs situated under that tree and shell beans again until they were all shelled, which took most of the rest of the afternoon.

Figure 25: Side of grandparent's house

Then God said, "Let the earth bring forth grass, the herb that yields seed, and the fruit tree that yields fruit according to its kind whose seed is in itself, on the earth" and it was so. (Genesis 1:11)

Figure 26: Front of grandparent's house

Then He said to His disciples, "The harvest is truly plentiful, but the laborers are few." (Matthew 9:37)

"But it was the opposite of what it's like now—the weather I mean. At the times we did that, mainly me and my mother, it was sunny and warm outside, but that oak tree provided all the shade we needed to make things comfortable."

Fred responded, "Yeah, Mag, what you describe is kinda like it was when I grew up, especially seeing my grandparents on occasion on the weekends. And like your grandfather, my granddad used to have a garden too. And after my grandmother prepared dinner, having cooked some of those butter beans and other vegetables along with maybe a pork roast, cornbread, and Kool-Aid, boy, was that some good eating!"

"Anyway, Fred, you know it's now approaching 1:00 in the morning, so we need to get some sleep."

After that they both stopped talking and drifted off. The wind, rain, and thunder continued for a little while longer in the morning before daybreak.

REFERENCE

"When you lie down, you will not be afraid; Yes, you will lie down and your sleep will be sweet." (Proverbs 3:24)

10. ANTICIPATING THE EXCURSION

The storm of the previous night had passed, and the last day on the island of Little Fiji began with the sun rising above the eastern horizon, promising a bright and clear day. One by one, members of the group started to come to the lobby. Gates and Courtney were the first to arrive there.

"Hey, Gates, take a look at this fireplace. It's really nice, don't you think?" Courtney asked.

"Yeah, everything about this place is nice. I really like it," he responded. "Well, Courtney, what do you want to do today? You know the ship is not going to leave until early tonight. So we have the whole day."

Courtney responded, "Well, here come Maggie and Fred. We can ask them what they have in mind."

When Maggie and Fred approached Gates and Courtney, Maggie took the initiative to speak first.

"Hello, you two. How was your night's rest?"

"Maggie, we rested great. We couldn't even tell if it was storming or not. We slept right through it," Courtney answered. "So how about you and Fred? Did you two sleep through it too?"

Maggie replied, "You know, Courtney, we were in bed but didn't go to sleep right away. It wasn't until well after midnight when finally went to sleep. In fact, it was right at 1:00 this morning when we dozed off."

Fred finally got to say something. "Yeah, Courtney, the storm didn't affect us that much."

Courtney replied, "Oh my. I know, Fred, you said the storm didn't affect you, but you two stayed awake so late; the storm must have kept you two up."

Maggie replied, "No, Courtney. It really didn't bother us. I'll tell you, I really enjoy summer storms although the stormy seas that we had last night were something different. We actually heard the roar of the ocean! At any rate, the rain and the howling wind have a different effect on me than on most people, I guess. What I'm saying is that instead of putting me to sleep, the storm last night had the effect of making me meditate on life. And that's what we did, me and Fred."

"That's very vague, Maggie. What exactly did you talk about?" Courtney asked.

Maggie said, "We talked about our time growing up."

"That's interesting," Courtney replied.

Gates jumped into the discussion. "How about you, Fred? Did you get a chance to think about some more material to put into your book?" Gates asked him.

Fred answered, "Yeah, Gates, I'm always thinking of something that I can write about. Hey, maybe I can do a story about you and Courtney. You two definitely have a compelling story. I mean maybe the time when you didn't believe in God, Gates, when you were an atheist? How about that? And, Courtney, wasn't there a time when you were an exotic dancer?"

Gates said, "Now, Fred, why do you want to bring all that mess up? That's a part of our history that's long gone. And I'll tell you what. God says that it's gone completely, erased from our slate of wrongdoings. I think the Bible calls it sin. But you know what, Fred? Not only those things but all the other things that we may have done that were not pleasing to God, He has erased. That's one of the first things that I've learned since becoming a believer. And if you repent

Figure 27: *Sins* **Being Erased with a Pencil.**

"Repent therefore and be converted, that your sins may be blotted out, so that times of refreshing may come from the presence of the Lord. (Acts 3:19)

and try to do better at whatever it is that's not pleasing to God, He'll help you overcome that issue. I'm a living witness that He'll do that. And you know what, Fred? I believe that's the case because we don't do those things anymore, that is, not having a belief in God and being active in the world's activities like Courtney and I once were a part of. So, Fred, I really don't want to talk about it." Noticing Gates' irritation as he gave his testimony, Fred said, "Okay, Gates. You don't have to get defensive about it. We're still friends."

Gates asked, "Hey, Maggie, how do you live with this guy? Everything is a story to him." Gates returned his attention to Fred. "But you're still my guy, Fred. And I respect you a lot, Maggie. You two are like family to me. And I know Courtney feels the same way."

"Amen," Courtney said confirming her husband's words.

Not long after Gates made those statements, Sandra and Katie walked into the lobby.

Maggie said, "Hey, you two. You slept in late, didn't you?"

Katie said, "Yeah, I got a lot of good rest, girl." Katie continued, directing her comments towards Sandra, "I think you did too, didn't you, Sandra?"

Sandra answered, "I really did, Katie. The storm didn't bother me at all."

Maggie asked, "Where is Wynn?"

Katie answered, "I don't know, girl. You know, I woke up and he was gone. He's probably somewhere with you know who."

Maggie responded, "Oh, yeah. I guess you're right. He's probably with Jeanie somewhere."

Courtney jumped back into the discussion. "Hey, you all, I want to clarify something by returning to what we were talking about before Sandra and Katie showed up. Listen, I know in my past life I was an exotic dancer, but I'm not now. I certainly haven't been like you, Fred, in church my whole life. And that's what's so great about God, that is, as a believer, God treats us all the same like His children—at least from the standpoint of loving each one of them. It's obvious that a parent might treat each of their children differently just because each child is different and requires different strategies of childrearing. But God is the same towards us. He treats us like individuals because we're all different. He does what's best for each one of us. You know each of us requires help from the Master in different ways, but thank God He loves us all the same."

Gates said, "Yeah, Courtney, you know you're a smart woman. That's one of the reasons I married you."

"Oh, Gates, those are some sweet words coming from you," Courtney said. She added, "But let's be honest, Gates. That's not the only reason you married me."

Gates said, "Yeah, I guess you're right, Courtney; your physical attributes didn't hurt either."

"Aw, let's be real, Gates," Fred added. "The girl was *fine* when you met her!"

Gates retorted, "Well, how would you know that, Fred? Those kinds of feelings towards my woman? I thought your heart was with Maggie when you were in Hawaii.

"Yeah, my heart was," Fred replied. "But I'll tell you what. Courtney was such a friend in Maggie's absence when I was out there."

"Well, exactly how close a friend was she, Fred?" Maggie asked her husband in a rather curious way.

"Oh, Maggie, how could you think such thoughts about Fred?" Courtney asked.

Fred didn't want to pursue the matter any further or open a can of worms, so he answered Maggie by saying, "Wait a minute, Courtney. Let me answer my wife. Now, Mag, don't you get defensive."

Before Fred could complete what he wanted to say, Maggie said, "*Defensive?*"

In order to soften his response to Maggie and to divert the

tone of the conversation, Fred tried to appease Maggie and offer a compliment to both Courtney and Gates.

"No, I'd never be defensive towards you, honey! And, yeah, Gates, and you too, Courtney. That's a lot of wisdom that you two just shared with all of us. But again you know Katie and Sandra, and I know you two just walked in. Let me tell you we carry on like this almost every Sunday after church at dinner at least during the times when we are able to meet."

The Manleys and the Mints had some lively discussions, and sometimes they would get into heated debates. But one thing they usually wouldn't debate was religion or their faith.

Gates interjected, "Well, Fred, sometimes we do talk about the scripture. Notice how I said it, everybody. We *talk about* scripture, not *debate* it. Well, you do know why there's no debate about it, don't you? Let me tell you why. It's because any discussion we have, my position is the right one. It turns out that my thoughts make the most sense! Am I right, Fred?"

Fred replied, "You, Gates, you're really funny sometimes—or try to be!"

Seeing where the discussion between Gates and Fred was headed, Maggie spoke up and said, "Okay, fellows, this discussion, if that's what you want to call it, is quickly headed downhill. We're not at one of our dinners where we do, I must admit, act kinda crazy. Sometimes like now on our vacation, let's take the high road, will you?"

"Okay, Mag," Fred responded. He turned his attention again to Gates and said, "And you know what, Gates? Maybe you should become a minister."

Gates replied, "Well, you know what, Fred? I'm thinking about doing just that. But the job I have now is hard enough with a lot of responsibility. But you know what, Fred? He did call me to do what I'm doing. I'm talking about on a professional level. And that is being the best businessman in the hotel industry that I can be."

Maggie shouted, "All right now, Gates. Yeah, I think you'd be a great minister. In fact, we're all ministers from the standpoint of trying to guide others in the right way. Anyway, I'm glad you ended up in the hotel business because, otherwise, I don't think we all would be on this trip, this cruise."

Gates went over and gave Maggie a high five and said to everyone, "You know, you all, that's why I respect this woman so much."

Maggie simply smiled in response to that comment.

REFERENCE

"For we are His workmanship, created in Christ Jesus for good works, which God prepared beforehand that we should walk in them." (Ephesians 2:10)

11. ADVENTURE LANDING

Gates had just finished a lively discussion with Maggie and her husband Fred when all of them realized they should accomplish something more useful.

Maggie said, "Everybody, we need to think about what we're going to do today—seriously. We don't leave until later tonight, and I have something in mind. I read about this mini theme park in the forest on the island. Let me be more specific. It has a roller coaster that goes through the forest. I'll get more information on it before lunch."

Maggie continued, "And another thing is that maybe we can eat lunch together and then go ride the roller coaster. I hope everyone has a positive opinion about the idea. I spoke to you, Katie, earlier about it, and, if I recall, you were a little hesitant. I think you said you saw a sign saying that 'you ride at your own risk.'"

Katie quickly spoke up. "Yes, I did see that sign, but I guess everything will be okay. Anyway, Maggie, I don't want to be left behind. I'm all for it."

Everyone agreed about going on this excursion. Maggie stressed the first order of business was to have lunch.

She said, "We should eat a very light lunch since we'll be going up and down on the roller coaster ride." She added, "I hope Wynn will show up for lunch too and go on the roller coaster with us."

§ § §

Wynn finally joined them for lunch. He had spent a good portion of the morning with Jeanie. When he heard about the group's plans, he was excited because it meant that there was good chance that he would see Jeanie again before they got back on the ship. Jeanie had told him earlier that her folks planned to take the roller coaster excursion. So when Wynn returned to the group, he was delighted to hear that they had similar plans. The only negative part of the whole thing was that so many other people also had signed up for the outing. Wynn figured that it would be unlikely to run into her in such a crowd. He said his goodbyes to Jeanie and went to join Maggie's group as Jeanie returned to Sheri and David.

Wynn was right about it being crowded. Maggie and their group took a shuttle from their hotel to the area where cruisers would board individual roller coaster cars. It was a short trip of only about thirty minutes.

When they arrived, Maggie commented, "Wow! Look at all these people. It looks like it's going to take us forever before our turn comes."

Large numbers of people stood waiting for their names to be called to get in their cars and take the ride. Maggie caught a glimpse of a boarding log that showed each string of connected cars could hold ten people. Since seven people in her group had signed up, she figured there would be more than enough room on any one of the connected cars. But she also realized that three seats would be available for others. She thought, *Where would the other three people come from to fill up the connecting cars that our group will be on*? She said quietly to herself, "No need to worry about that now."

With those thoughts, Maggie saw the next connecting coaster cars arrive in front of the group.

"Wow! What an interesting setup," Sandra said, not speaking to anyone in particular, as she saw the makeup of the roller coaster they soon would be on. The setup consisted of five two-seat coaster cars connecting to one another. The seven persons in Maggie's group that would board these connecting cars were by now lined up in the alphabetical order of family last names.

Figure 28: Roller coaster cars

Whenever I am afraid, I will trust in You.

(Psalm 56:3)

Maggie hollered, "Now listen for your name to be called so we all can board these five connecting cars. An attendant is over there to help in the boarding process. So, everybody, this is the boarding order from the list given to me. Now come on and get up in your car when I call your name.

"Sandra, you'll be first because your last name comes up first among names in alphabetical order. And since you don't have a partner and the other party of three hasn't arrived yet, you can go to the second car from the front and sit in one of those seats."

Sandra asked, "Hey, Maggie, what about the two seats in the first car in front of me?"

Maggie said, "Well, Sandra, the group of three that hasn't arrived yet will take those two seats, and the third person in that party will sit beside you. They should be here soon. And if they're not, they simply get left!"

After that comment, Sandra followed Maggie's instructions and got in her seat.

Maggie continued to call their names for boarding. She said, "Okay, the next persons to board, again in alphabetical order, are the Lyons, Katie and Wynn; you two can go and take your seats in the third car behind where Sandra is."

Maggie continued, "Now the Manleys, Gates and Courtney. You two can get on in the fourth car."

After they boarded Maggie said, "Now the last ones to board are the Mints, me and Fred. We'll be in the fifth car, so Fred you can go ahead and get on, and I'll get myself seated in just a second."

As Maggie gave instructions, she said, "As I said, Sandra, someone will be sitting with you once that party of three gets here. Also, on your side is a brake lever, so if there's a need to stop the coaster cars from rolling, you'll be in control of that."

Maggie saw on the boarding log that the family of three, whose name was Logan, would fill the remaining two seats, the front two seats with Sandra being right behind them. That family hadn't arrived yet.

The attendant said to Maggie, "We'll give that party of three another two minutes to arrive, and, if they're not here by then, you all can leave without them."

When the attendant finished, Maggie said, "Well, you heard 'em. We'll have to wait a bit. And by the way the name of that party of three is the Logans."

With that bit of information, all of a sudden Katie heard her son shout with joy. He said loudly, "The Logans? Why, that's Jeanie and her folks!"

Katie asked, "Wynn, what's wrong with you shouting like that?" She added, "Well, I guess you are excited if that is in fact the Logans that we know."

Wynn replied, "Yeah, mom. That's what I'm saying. The group just in front of us in those first two cars is Jeanie and her folks! Yeah, their last name is Logan, so they will be just ahead of us in that first car since we're seated in alphabetical order. And Jeanie will probably be sitting in the second car right in front of us there beside Miss Sandra. Look, I can prove it."

He spoke loudly to Maggie, who was sitting in the back. "Miss Maggie, could I see the boarding log that you just read from to show my mother?"

Maggie replied, "Well, sure, Wynn. Here it is." She handed the document to Courtney just ahead of her to pass to him. She mentioned, "Well, what do you know? It still will be a little time before that family gets here."

Wynn took the boarding log and showed it to Katie, who took a glance and verified what her son was saying. "Yeah, Maggie. Wynn's right. The Logans are just ahead of us."

"Well, that's interesting. But where are they?" Katie asked. "Now that's interesting because we're getting ready to go! They're gonna get left if they're not here soon."

Maggie agreed on both counts.

Hopeful that he would see Jeanie again, Wynn said, "We've *got to* wait for them. They'll be here."

As the last call was being made to get on board, Sheri, Jeanie, and David walked frantically to get there and take their seats.

Once they arrived Maggie said, "Sheri, we're so surprised to see you, but Wynn remembered your last name. Anyway, you all just made it. And hello to you too, Jeanie and David."

After Sheri and her clan returned the greeting, Maggie said, pointing toward the front of the five connected cars, "See those first two seats up there in the first car and the seat beside Sandra in the car behind it? They're yours so you can go ahead and take them and we can get moving."

Without directly responding to Maggie, Sheri said, "Come on, David. Let's take the two seats in the first car, and, Jeanie, you can sit there with Sandra in the second car behind us. And hello, Sandra," Sheri added as they rushed to get to their seats.

Sandra responded, "Hello, Sheri. And, Jeanie, go ahead and sit here beside me."

Wynn was so happy to see Jeanie, who took her seat just in front of him next to Sandra.

Sheri, David, and Jeanie were as surprised as anyone to see Maggie's group. After getting situated, Sheri turned around and said to them, "I'm sure glad to see you all again—especially in this situation. It's going to be pretty scary!"

Overwhelmed with joy, Maggie, who sat in the back seat, yelled over everyone, "We're glad to see you again, Sheri! Well, I think everyone is in their seats now, and we're all going to be in for a ride. So hold on to your seats!"

§ § §

Sandra had mixed emotions about the impending coaster ride. She knew the ride through the forest of Little Fiji would be thrilling, but having David this close brought back her recent experiences with him. Her interlude with him left her anxious and ashamed, but she couldn't deny there had been a sense of connection with him emotionally. With Jeanie sitting beside her and Sheri and David directly in front, her thoughts raced.

Once everyone was on board, Gates said to Wynn, "Young fella, let me have that boarding list to verify that everyone is in their correct positions."

Wynn gave to the log to Gates, who reviewed the document and confirmed what Wynn had said.

"Yeah, Wynn's right. The Logans are correctly seated there in the front."

After overhearing Gates, David shouted, "Okay now. Let's get rolling!"

Gates continued to examine the document as he turned around in his seat. "And, yeah, we're listed as being just ahead of you all," he said to Maggie and Fred. "Well, Maggie, I have to notify my hotel administration of this adventure too, but everything seems fine, and we're ready to go."

Wynn said, "I'm so glad you're here, Jeanie, sitting next to Miss Sandra."

Sandra just sat there, overwhelmed by her feelings and thoughts. David turned around, smiled, and briefly said to her, "Hello, Sandra."

Sandra looked down and whispered to Jeanie, "Are you

comfortable?"

Jeanie replied, "Yes, Miss Sandra."

Katie was less than thrilled about being near David, but she liked Sheri and Jeanie a lot. She had become particularly fond of Sheri because she had grown to know and appreciate her as a person during the trip to the mall back in Bermuda. But she couldn't get David's uncaring demeanor and actions out of her mind.

Maggie said, "Sandra, are you okay riding in that second car from the front? I say that because based on the drawing of the coaster cars, that's the one with the emergency brakes on it. So in an emergency, you'll be the one who will stop all these cars from moving. So you're good with that?"

"Oh, yes, Maggie. I'm fine," Sandra assured her. "Besides, I love having this kind of control," she said in jest. "But let's face it, you all; nothing is likely to happen."

To herself she thought, *Why am I around this man again?*

With everyone in their places, Maggie yelled to the attendant, "I think we're ready to roll!"

Everyone nodded their heads in agreement, but at that point no one had a choice. They were about to go roller coasting!

§ § §

The string of coaster cars soon began to move, and all the chatter ceased. The only concern now was trying to enjoy the adventure as much as possible without being scared out of their wits. As the five-car, ten-seat coaster made its way up the track taking them high above the forest, even a glance downward was terrifying.

Courtney whispered loudly, "It's so far down, you all, too far down for a soft landing if we were to fall into that forest down there."

"Oh, girl, don't talk about falling," Sandra chimed in.

Maggie said, "Aw, Courtney, don't be such a scaredy-cat! This ride will be a breeze. Just sit back and enjoy it."

Maggie continued in a reassuring tone, "Yes, an adventure landing down there should be the last thing on your mind. You all keep the faith."

Courtney responded in jest, "Okay but we're just so far above the forest. And look at the large body of water over there. We're going over that too? *Oh, boy!*"

§ § §

As the five cars slowly approached the summit, the view on both sides got increasingly spectacular. Nothing but forested terrain covered the landscape. They could still hear birds chirping as a slight breeze wafted across their faces. The cars in front reached the summit and were ready to descend the first of several declines of the track route. The initial descent seemed the most frightening. The track on which the cars were rolling was attached to solid ground, and they had gone up an extremely steep hill with a sharp decline on both sides.

Beyond the summit, the track lay atop a tall support structure similar to a railroad bridge extending high above the surface. This was necessary because they were approaching a river that flowed through the Little Fiji forest. Sandra, for one, caught the brilliance of the environment as she snapped several pictures prior to the rapid movement of the coaster. From that vantage point, they could see for miles as the river emptied into the ocean. Even the cruise ship was visible at the dock in the distance.

Suddenly at the peak of the hill, the lead car, the one with Sheri and David in it, began its descent. A loud jerking sound frightened Sandra so much that she panicked and pulled the lever on the side of her car. This had the effect of stopping the four remaining cars from going further and caused the lead car to detach from the others and start to plummet down the hillside. Its wheels had come loose from the track beneath it, so the car and its occupants tumbled hundreds of feet from near the summit downward towards the forest floor. It landed in the river far below them.

Everyone in the group screamed in shock at what had just transpired. Sheri and David were gone. Their coaster car sank into the river until it was completely submerged. Jeanie became hysterical, and other members of the group were in a state of disbelief. She was screaming at the top of her voice.

"Mom! Mom!" she shouted through choked sobs. She couldn't bear the thought of losing another parent after the loss of her father. "My God, my God," she repeated, wailing.

Maggie and her friends watched in horror as Sheri and David's car sank into the waters. Jeanie only had Sandra beside her, in disbelief like the others, to hold her and provide some degree of comfort.

During all the commotion, Gates shouted, "Now no one move because our cars aren't stable. We could all tumble down at any moment just like the car that Sheri and David were in." He continued, "Behind us an emergency car is coming to get us. Until that happens, don't anyone move."

Maggie clung to her husband for dear life. "Fred, Fred, I can't look down," she said. "I'm so frightened."

Courtney and Gates and Katie and Wynn embraced each other tightly in an effort to remain calm and still. Wynn so much wanted to get to Jeanie, but Katie held on to her son so that he would not cause another catastrophe.

Gates told everyone that moving in any way was out of the question. One slight shift could tilt the cars and send them tumbling to their fate. Finally, Wynn couldn't take it anymore. He struggled with his mother to free himself and somehow go to Jeanie.

And the unthinkable happened. The other four cars began to

plunge down the embankment. They crashed just prior to landing completely in the water. Their cars were only partially submerged. Everyone went into panic mode, screaming and completely out of their wits.

Shock overtook their senses, and the next time of conscious reality for each of them was back on the cruise liner, where emergency medical personnel had taken them.

When all the other cruisers gradually were led back onto the ship, two precious souls were missing.

REFERENCE

"Though He slay me, yet will I trust Him." (Job 13:15)

12. *"EYE HAS NOT SEEN, NOR EAR HEARD..."*

When Maggie regained consciousness, she was back on board the cruise liner heading towards New York. She was sitting on a sofa in a large lobby area of the ship with John, her first husband, right there beside her.

She said, "John, what do you think about the event that we had last night, our wedding anniversary banquet?"

Maggie's mind had traveled back to a time long before she thought about going on a cruise. She recalled resuming her duties as First Lady of Faith Methodist Church where John was the pastor.

John replied, "It was a grand event. I was really surprised that you would pull something like that together. You know how much I love being in the limelight. But you know what? More attention should have been given to my father. Without him, I wouldn't be nearly where I am now, having the status and recognition in the Detroit community."

Maggie responded, "Yeah, I hear you, John, but you deserve it. The congregation really loves the energy you bring in presenting the Word. And as far as the community, I think a lot of people appreciate your service."

As Maggie spoke, Fred walked into the lobby and recognized John.

"Hello, John," he said.

"Hey there, Fred," John replied.

Fred said, "You know, Mag, I just came from the top deck, and the scenery as we left Little Fiji was just magnificent!" He added, "And, John, I felt the same way when I left Hawaii to return to Chicago. But, you know, what I remember most about my stay there was when I first met you. Remember? When I was about to have dinner with Maggie? Boy, were you upset! Well, I guess you had a right to be. If someone was talking to my wife like that, I guess I would feel the same way."

John responded, "Yeah, I did go berserk, didn't I? And, Mag, I hope I didn't hurt your arm when I pulled you away from Fred that night."

Maggie said, "No, John. You didn't hurt me. But I must admit you made quite a scene. And that was our first experience with Gates. Remember?"

John replied, "Yeah, Gates really came down on me. But, believe me, I really deserved it. And I had no right to call him names, like baldy."

Gates and Courtney walked into the lobby and heard John and Fred talking about him. Knowing that he was the focus of their discussion, he said, "Hey, you two, I heard my name called."

John said, "Yeah, Gates, Fred and I were recalling the time when you pulled me away as I was confronting him and Maggie.

"Oh, yeah," Gates began. "It was a very rough situation. You know, John, at the time you really caused a scene. But, hey, man, you had a right too. After all, you saw someone who you thought was messing with your woman."

Maggie added, "Well, Gates, you have to remember that Fred and I go way back to when we were in college. In fact, that's where I met Fred at that school social after a basketball game at MCCU."

John said, "That's about the time I returned to Flint from divinity school and started to help my father where he was pastor at Mark Methodist."

Maggie added, "As you know, John, we go back even further even before you went off to divinity school. You know we grew up together in Mark Methodist."

John said, "Yeah, Maggie, and I remember playing with your little sister Sadie and some of your other siblings too. Speaking of Sadie, she was a mess—kind of contrary as I remember her."

As Maggie recalled her sister, Sadie walked into the lobby.

She said, "Did I hear my name called? You all know I haven't been on a cruise before. This is really nice! You all need to give this place some life. We're not at a funeral you know! And where is that sister of mine, Maggie? I heard that she is the reason we're on this cruise."

Maggie saw Sadie and said, "Hello, Sade. Let me correct you. I wasn't the reason why we're all on this cruise; it's my friend Gates. Yeah, he's the one that's a hotel owner and he made arrangements for a group of us to go with him on the cruise to Bermuda."

Sadie said to her sister, "Aw, Bermuda, that place is really nice!"

Sadie was there with them in spirit. No one could sense her except for Maggie during her meditative time on the beach after her walk with Erin. Maggie perceived her sister in the spirit while she was alone. She felt connected to her, and they were able to commune with one another in the spiritual realm. Maggie also communicated with her mother Mensie in the same way at that time. It was so pleasant and peaceful. Maggie had a spiritual connection with her mother prior to her passing although there were some conflicts going on while she remained in the physical. Maggie was tempted to tell her mother to mind her own business when she observed Mensie trying so hard to get her date John Jr. while Maggie was more interested in Fred, that basketball player she met in college. But out there on the beach, there were no such distractions.

Maggie said, "You know, Sade, we had a brief talk back in Bermuda when I was on the beach. I looked up and kind of imagined that I was having a conversation with you."

Sadie said, "Yeah, I was right there, Mag. Even though you couldn't see me, I could see everything that you were doing, including your time spent with that lady. I believe her name is Erin."

"Yeah, Sade, my friend's name that lives in Bermuda is Erin!" Maggie continued, "Oh, Sade, you don't know how much I would have wanted you to meet her—right there on the beach."

Sadie replied, "But, Mag, I was there, like I said, in spirit. I know all about her. And you know what? She knows all about me too because we have a like spirit."

Sadie offered Maggie some spiritual insight. "You know what, Mag, in the spiritual dimension, I would know more about your friend Erin than even you did there on the beach, being with her in your physical body. But I realize that you two connected even spiritually. But, let me tell you, there's an effort in communicating with someone spiritually when you're a part of a physical, materialistic world and susceptible to all the concerns and distractions it brings. We might think we know someone, but it's difficult to connect totally with their spirit, to know what they are really about."

Maggie responded, "Yeah, you're right, Sade, but that's where God comes in. He's the only one that knows all about us. The rest of us don't really know each other like that because we don't have total knowledge of a person's spirit like God does. And God knows us like that totally, that is, knows our spirit totally, because He made us. But we, as His children, are getting there. As a matter of fact, in the scripture it says that on the day of our transition from a physical existence to one that is spiritual we'll be like Him."

"Wow, what insight you have into the spirit, Mag," Sadie said.

"And let me tell you something else, Mag," Sadie continued. "I was aware of things way back—even at my funeral. I had transitioned into my spiritual body and was aware of you, mom, dad and our other siblings and how sad it was for everyone. There I was lying in the casket. My body was dead, motionless, but my spirit had been released, and the real me, my spirit, was as alive as ever. I guess you all didn't realize that what you saw in that casket wasn't the real me. My spirit was very much alive. I don't even remember what happened, what caused my transition," Sadie said, not recalling that she was murdered in a case of mistaken identity.

"I had no control over the physical body you saw lying there, a lifeless body of flesh. But, believe me, I was more than alive, at least your concept of being alive in your physical body. I was aware of everything, including your thoughts. And so I was aware of your hurt, the hurt of losing someone you love. I just utilized my ability to choose not to recall your hurt, because I loved you too much, Mag," Sadie told her sister. "But I'm in a perfectly happy situation now as well as at that time, because I understand that you will ultimately come to the knowledge that I have after your own transition."

While not completely understanding all that Sadie had just communicated, Maggie said, "Okay, Sade; that's great, but let me tell you how important Erin has been to me, and I'm sure to others that have been around her. An important thing that Erin has taught me is that we who are still in our physical bodies also have that spirit which can communicate directly to God. And it is as through that spirit, that is, that spirit part of our being, is able to connect with Him."

Sadie added, "Well, you know what, Mag? That same spirit can communicate with anybody in the flesh if they've gained a knowledge of Him and believe in Him. And if you don't have that knowledge, this kind of communication may not make a lot of sense to the average person. But the exciting thing, Mag, is that we're not average! In fact, God tells us that not only are we not average, we are peculiar, a peculiar people in service for Him and His purposes on the earth. And I think that scripture is in First Peter."

Sadie continued, "And I think that's the key. You have to believe, and I mean sincerely believe, Mag. I guess what I'm saying is that if you believe that Jesus lived and is in fact alive right now, His Spirit can connect with our spirits, and that's when amazing things start to happen. So, Mag, that's what happened there on the beach when we were communicating with each other, with each other's spirit."

Maggie said, "You know, Sade, I agree with you. And so you know what? I believe that God being spirit Himself was right there in our midst!

Sadie responded, "You got that right, girl!"

As Maggie conversed with Sadie, John and Gates stood off to the side, talking about their confrontation back in Hawaii as well as Gates' clash with David in Bermuda.

John said, "Well, Gates, I understand you put your security background to work when you had another confrontation, one similar to what we had back in Hawaii, with one of the guests at this resort in Bermuda. I think his name was David."

Gates replied, "Yeah, John, I had some issues with David all right. And like you said, it was quite a bit of commotion that we had there in Bermuda, not unlike what we experienced back in Hawaii. But you know what? That's water over the dam or spilled milk as they say sometimes."

John replied, "Having gone to divinity school and having been a pastor, I've studied the Word a lot. And you do know that the scripture says that we should only think on things that are good, pure, and holy? I think that verse of scripture is found in Philippians 4. And, let me tell you, Gates, there was nothing holy about the confrontation that you had with David. But I want to look at the bright side, so I have to admit that he has nice support with Sheri and Jeanie."

Fred chimed into the discussion. "Yeah, Gates, look how God turned your life around, and at one time you didn't even believe He existed!"

After John and Gates had talked with each other and Fred had added his two cents, David himself burst into the room.

He said, "I heard someone call my name. Well, I want to tell you all that I'm here now! And my people are here too. And I want to tell you all, Sheri cares a lot about you, about Maggie and the rest of you too. And Sheri's daughter Jeanie can't seem to keep her hands off Katie's son Wynn. And by the way, Katie, I regret what happened that night when I tried to take my seat from you at dinner, you know, when I came in late? I was wrong and, to be honest with you, I only wanted that seat so that I could talk to Sandra, who was sitting beside me. Yeah, I've come to my senses and realize what a wonderful gift I have in Sheri, and I'll try to show more respect to her with God helping me."

Sandra, who was standing nearby, said, "You know, David, I've learned a lot too, and I think that's what you're saying." She continued, "You know, you all, God can forgive me. Let me rephrase that. He has forgiven me of the many bad things that I've done. And because of that I'll have to forgive you, David, as well as forgiving others who've wronged me. And I want to tell you, since that time when you wronged me, I've forgiven you of your actions. Hey, I also realize that I wasn't totally faultless during that episode either!"

Sheri said, "Yeah, Sandra, David explained to me everything, and I want to let you know that we're all good with you."

David added, "Thanks, Sheri, for saying that, and thank you too, Sandra, for forgiving me. And I want to tell everyone that I've grown to like everyone here, to love everyone, in fact, and especially Gates who I've talked to a lot since that confrontation with you, Katie, and I found that he was a lot like me before he was converted. But let me tell all of you, I'm not there yet, and I have a lot to learn about the faith."

Gates added, "Yeah, David, we all have a lot to learn yet about doing what's right."

Maggie said, "Yes, David, Gates and Courtney, his wife, are testimonies of how God can turn lives around. Courtney has talked about how she has overcome so much in her life, and you can too. I realize that you haven't arrived to where you're supposed to be, but again none of us have."

After Maggie had spoken those words of wisdom, David took in as much as he could in his discussions with everyone assembled there.

§ § §

While everyone was talking, Wynn and Jeanie slipped away to the top deck again. They talked about all kinds of things with one notable exception. They didn't discuss their experience at the roller coaster and their frightful landing, tumbling down the hill. Jeanie told Wynn that the pastor of her church spoke about moving forward in life and not focusing on past events that you can do nothing about. Jeanie explained that her pastor's motto was to look straight ahead in pursuit of your goals, aspirations that matched the talents God gave you.

She added, "My pastor also said, Wynn, that you can have anything you want as long as you believe that you'll get it. And I certainly believe that, Wynn, because I've always wanted to be with you, and look at us now! After all that we've been through, I'm right here with you."

§ § §

Erin walked into the lobby and everyone in Maggie's group was startled.

"What in the world are you doing here?" Sandra said.

Erin answered, "I'm here to introduce to everyone the man and the lady of the evening. I'm presenting to everyone Mr. and Mrs. Brown, Mensie and Matthew. Come on out here and show everyone what you can do!"

Matthew and Mensie came into the lobby dressed in shag dancing attire. The two of them began to dance to the tune of "Heat Wave." They shagged all around the center of the lobby with everyone cheering and singing along.

Maggie was so happy to see her father dancing. She vividly recalled the time after the fall when he became paralyzed. But she also remembered him promising her that she would see him walk again. She had not really believed his words at the time, choosing to feel sorry for him and wallow in self-pity. But now she was witnessing him not only walking but dancing the night away with her mother Mensie.

And Maggie was overjoyed to see her mother so vibrant and full of life as she'd always known her. She was enjoying herself instead of being pre-occupied with what others were doing.

The volume of the music rose to a pitch that was too loud even for Sandra's taste. But she sang along with everyone else anyway as Mensie and Matthew danced.

When Maggie saw her parents dancing in her dream, that's when she woke up. She remembered clearly going on the vacation of a lifetime, a cruise to Bermuda. She recalled every detail of the planning and execution of that trip as if it really happened.

Maggie lay there now fully awake, looking up through the skylight Fred had installed at what was still a starlit night. Fred slept soundly beside her. She said quietly to herself, "I can't wait 'til tomorrow to tell Fred about the dream I just had. Speaking directly to her Creator, she added, "I now realize that, as You say in Your word, Lord, 'Eye has not seen nor ear heard' what You have in store for Your children, for those who overcome, for those who are willing to believe and to act on that word."

Maggie could hardly to wait to share her dream, so she decided to wake Fred and tell him.

§ § §

When Maggie first awakened, she moved as little as possible because she remembered Fred saying not to wake him until morning. But she wanted to share the dream with him while it remained fresh in her mind. She gave him a little nudge and softly said, "Fred, Fred, are you awake?"

Fred growled, yawned a little, not fully alert, and sarcastically said, "Well, I am now." He asked, "Well, what is it? I thought I said not to wake me up 'til morning."

"Sorry to awaken you, Fred, but I have to tell you about this dream I had."

Fred could hardly believe her words. "Sure, Mag, you didn't mean to wake me up. But now I am awake, so what was your dream about?" he asked.

"Glad you asked, honey," she responded.

When Maggie felt certain Fred was fully awake, she continued, "I dreamed that all of us went on a cruise that Gates had arranged. It was so real, Fred. Gates had organized a cruise to Bermuda and needed four couples to come along with him in order to make the trip work. It had something to do with his hotel administration doing a promotion. Anyway, to make a long story short, some of our friends came along to join my group. So, in addition to Gates and Courtney, the other couples that came along with me and you included my college roommate Katie and her son Wynn and Sandra. Now I know that's only three couples, but I had called Erin, our host in Bermuda, and she said she'd be willing to partner with Sandra to make up a fourth couple."

Fred said, "Well, that's great, Maggie."

Before he could say anything else, Maggie quickly added, "But there's a lot more, Fred, because there was another couple that joined us. It was a guy with a lady and daughter. The guy's name was David, and you know what he tried to do, Fred? He hit on Sandra! Can you imagine that?"

Fred responded, "Well, actually, Mag, I can imagine that because, you know, Sandra is an attractive woman. I can see why any man would want to do that if he could."

Maggie responded in disgust, saying, "Fred! I'm surprised you'd say such a thing! I mean, the guy was already in a commitment! And his friend—her name was Sheri—was such a nice lady too."

Fred replied, "I'm only kidding, Mag."

Maggie tried to continue talking to Fred, hoping that he would take her more seriously.

"I'm still surprised at you, Fred. Anyway, let me get back to what I was saying. But listen," Maggie said. "I'll make this short, but let me tell you. We all ended up going to this small island on our way back to New York. While there, we all decided to ride on a roller coaster through a forest, and…and…" Maggie paused. Getting emotional, she continued, "It crashed with all of us in the roller coaster cars, Fred!"

She began to cry uncontrollably. Fred handed his wife some tissue.

"Here, Mag. Dry your face so you can continue."

Maggie replied, "Thanks." Slowly she started to regain her composure.

After Fred asked if she was okay, Maggie, now able to continue talking, said, "So let me finish. You know, Fred, the weirdest thing happened after that crash. We all apparently died and went to heaven, and it was so peaceful there."

Maggie continued, "One reason it was so peaceful, Fred, as I remember in the dream, had to do with Sandra. I remember her telling everyone how this lady in Bermuda—we knew of her as Erin— how Erin had given her spiritual advice and had somehow helped her overcome her ailment, her terminal condition. Remember how I told you that mom had given me all the details of Sandra's experience, and Sandra herself told me directly about those events that she had mentioned to mom earlier."

Maggie continued, "And speaking of mom, Fred, in the dream I also had a vision of her dancing with my father. I couldn't believe it! My father on his feet again dancing after having seen him paralyzed from the fall he had trying to hang those Christmas lights for my mother at our house. I didn't think I'd ever see him walk again. And not only that, but I had a vision of my sister Sadie as well as my other siblings. It was like a grand reunion. We were so peaceful and happy. All I saw myself doing was reminiscing about old times growing up and about when I went off to college and met you, Fred. But it's kind of interesting that in the dream I recalled only the pleasant times, not the challenging times that I had in my life, and Lord knows there were many of those."

Maggie figured that Fred was tired of hearing all that transpired in her dream, so she said, "Well, I know that's a lot, Fred, but what an interesting dream. Now let's go back to sleep, and I'll be sure to fix that hot breakfast you talked about before you first dozed off."

Now wide awake, Fred wanted to continue the conversation. After she decided she had told him enough of her dream, he said, "Oh no, Mag. You woke me up and now you'll have to listen to me."

"Okay, Fred, so what is it?" she asked.

"By the way I'm still looking forward to that hot breakfast!" he said with a smile. "Anyway, what you told me about in your dream reminds me of the time we met. Remember at the social back at MCCU after the basketball game? Before that I was lost. I didn't know what I wanted to do with my life. But when I met you, all that changed. I became a new person! And you know what? Your spiritual guidance helped me as much as anything. I began to know God in a special way, in a way I had not known Him before, even though I've attended church all my life."

Fred continued, "What I'm saying, Mag, is that..." He paused for a moment as he too became emotional. "During the first part of my life, I knew about God but didn't understand that He could be involved with my personal life. I mean, I began to realize that I could pray and ask Him for His help in solving a problem, any problem that I might have. Yeah, that was the second part of my life, having a personal relationship with the Master! But let me tell you, Mag, that second part of my life hasn't been easy. I mean, a part of me still wanted to do my own thing, and that's why I decided to go to Hawaii, leaving you behind back in Detroit after graduating early from MCCU. Now I realize that it wasn't such a good decision. Being away from you, the love of my life, was difficult, and you ended up marrying someone else, your childhood sweetheart John."

Fred continued, "Mag, I never really got over you being married to John. But after he died and I returned to Chicago, I tried to get back with you and fortunately it all worked out. And here we are married to each other!"

As Fred talked with Maggie, he delivered a more significant truth about their quest to find heaven on earth, to be with each other.

"Mag, that night back at MCCU I believe I found my heaven on earth when I found you."

Maggie interjected, "Yeah, it has worked out between me and you, being married and all. But something I learned back at my home church of Mark Methodist was that everything ultimately works out for the good if you love God and if you are in His perfect will. And, in a strange way, while it was very difficult to see you leave for Hawaii when you did, my reconnecting with John worked out best for me at the time, because I gained a lot of experience that I would not have gained otherwise. And something else Fred, I really grew to love John, to love him very much, even though I know I told you about his abuse. But the abuse wasn't life-threatening or anything like that. But I wanted more attention than he could give me or at least was willing to give me at the time, and it hurt a lot. This is one of the reasons you and I ended up together that night in Hawaii when John confronted you as you and I were about to eat dinner. I was as much to blame as anyone because I was married to him but was involved with you. So I've had my own issues concerning relationships, the Lord only knows."

Fred replied, "Yeah, Mag, I understand some of what you're saying, but hindsight is always 20/20. We just have to move forward with our life. And I learned this much from you, Mag, moving forward not only means trying to find that heaven on earth in this life but also realizing that the real heaven comes only after our transition from these physical bodies to our spiritual awareness of everything, the kind of spiritual awareness you said you had in your dream."

Fred continued, "And awareness is knowing the reality of being with God in spirit. You see, Mag, that's the third part of what I was telling you about earlier, the trilogy of my life if you want to call it that. And I say that because of the reason you woke me up in the first place, to tell me about the dream you had. Amidst all the negative events you said occurred with the roller coaster crash and all of us having died because of it, the most exciting thing about what you mentioned was that you experienced heaven with all your friends and relationships having perfect peace. Yeah, that's the culmination of it all."

Maggie responded, "Yeah, what you're saying is true, Fred. Still, while I envisioned what I think heaven could be like, we have to admit the fruition of that trilogy, that is, the reality of what the Bible says, is even more exciting. And now I am satisfied with His likeness, with what I experienced in that dream. Despite the reality of what I experienced in the dream, we still see through a dim glass, as the scripture says, and can't quite picture everything that God has in store for us. That is to say, Fred, 'no eye has seen, nor ear heard' the good things that He has prepared for them who love and believe Him."

After those comments, both Fred and Maggie drifted off to sleep again, hoping to have more pleasant dreams, and, for Fred, to have that hot breakfast in the morning!

REFERENCE

"As for me, I shall behold Your face in righteousness' I will be satisfied with Your likeness when I awake." (Psalm 17:15)

ABOUT THE AUTHOR

William Porter is the author of four inspirational books. He has produced two non-fictional works and two fictional novels. Go to his website at WilliamPorterLife.com to review the books he has written. The latest in a series of fictional novels include "Heaven Can't Wait: Or Can it? Dreams of Love, Deceit, and Hope," and a follow-up to that book is "Heaven Can't Wait: Or Can it?: THE SEQUEL." His current book, "Heaven Can't Wait: Or Can it? THE FRUITION is a follow-up to the story presented in the SEQUEL.

Don't miss William Porter's next book—a continuation of the Heaven Can't Wait Series! You'll be going to "The Island of Love." Don't miss what's in store for Maggie and her friends on this adventure!

COMING in the Fall of 2021

Don't miss other volumes in the *Heaven Can't Wait or Can It?* series

Heaven Can't Wait or Can It? Dreams of Love, Deceit and Hope

This novel is the first in the series as lead character Maggie and her friends seek their "Heaven on Earth." However, while making their earthly journey, there are many pitfalls in pursuing this goal.

Heaven Can't Wait or Can It? The Sequel

This novel is a follow-up to the first in this series. Maggie and her friends continue the saga of trying to find "Heaven on Earth" while living in an imperfect world.